About *Roadhouse Affairs*

December, 1930 — when the high times of the Roaring Twenties were sinking fast into the blues of the Great Depression and the mostly tolerated crime of rum-running and selling bootleg alcohol during Prohibition was all the rage, California's San Mateo Coast was jumping. Despite hard times, there were still plenty of people who had money enough for the good life. Socialites, high-stakes gamblers, and movie stars flocked to the fashionable speakeasies, especially along the coasts, where real hooch could still be run in by night, Roulette wheels kept spinning, poker games shuffled along, and the dames were as gorgeously outfitted as ever. There, parties could continue virtually uninterrupted. At Frank's Roadhouse in Half Moon Bay, the good life is in full swing. Until a blackmailer begins targeting Frank's wealthy and well-known clientele.

Though retired from the American Detective Agency and living an unencumbered life in Mexico, The Detective's unique skills are required to ferret out the blackmailer without either scaring away the rich and famous clientele at The Roadhouse, or alerting the Roadhouse owner, Frank Torres, who may be involved in the scam himself. Torres is wary about having The Detective as a guest at his Roadhouse, but he is a paying customer. Torres suspects ulterior motives, something beyond a mere vacation.

Discretion — even subterfuge — is imperative, especially since the Agency and its wealthy client, socialite Alma Spreckels, widow of the sugar magnate, have no idea which people at the Roadhouse are part of the complicated blackmailing scheme. All anyone knows for certain is that members of several wealthy families who stayed at the Roadhouse have been *marks,* and Mrs. Spreckels is paying big money to have it stopped — to safeguard her son, who's one of the victims. Whether anyone else also benefits from her intervention is irrelevant to "Big Alma," so long as her son, the heir to the vast Spreckels' fortune, is protected.

The Agency Chief calls The Detective out of retirement to do this one last job. A perilous one involving criminals who are willing to prey on socialites and movie stars wealthy and courageous enough to fight back against blackmail.

Bootleggers, socialites, movie stars, blackmail. It's a dangerous cocktail. And no one can guess how it will taste going down.

Other Books by Newton Love

How the Strong Survive

La Voie des Braves
(French translation of *How the Strong Survive)*

No Accounting for Taste (A Nick Schavers' Mystery, Book 1)

When Dead Cats Bounce (A Nick Schavers' Mystery, Book 2)

Odd & Odder: A Collection of Sensuality, Satire, & Suspense

Roadhouse Affairs

a novel

Newton Love

RockWay Press, LLC
NM • USA

E-Book ISBN 9781940206905
Trade Paper ISBN 9781940206899
LCCN   2014936715

• Cover Artwork "Onslow Avenue 2010" © 2010, 2014 by John Hannah. Used with the artist's gracious permission.

• Frank's Place (Roadhouse) vintage photographs, and Moss Beach Distillery contemporary photographs © 2014 by Moss Beach Distillery. Used with the MBD owners' kind permission.

• Original description of Frank's Place (Roadhouse) and of The Ghost of the Lady in Blue © 2014 by Moss Beach Distillery. Used with permission.

• Revisions of original description of Frank's Place and Ghost of Lady in Blue for this novel © 2014 by Alexandria Szeman.

• Section divider designed by Denis Barbulot (collection #16672940), provided by 123RF.com (sister company of Inmagine.com). Used with permission.

• Cover design by Alexandria Szeman & RockWay Press, LLC. © 2014 Alexandria Szeman & RockWay Press, LLC.

• Interior design by RockWay Press, LLC. © 2014 Alexandria Szeman & RockWay Press, LLC.

• Author Photograph © 2014 by Nance Love.

Publisher's Note: This novel is a work of fiction. Though historical figures, places, and incidents appear in this novel, they are used in artistic ways by appearing with fictitious characters, places, and incidents that are wholly the product of the author's imagination; any resemblance to actual persons (living or dead), remarks, quotes, events, organizations, or locales is entirely coincidental or is used fictitiously/artistically.

Visit our Web site at RockWay Press.com

for
Nance Love,
artist, mentor, and partner

You are the "green lantern"
into which I plug my life

Acknowledgments

To my Oxford chum Garry "Gaz" Lockeley. I met Gaz in St. Louis, Missouri, working aerospace in the 1990s. He was the intellectual heir to the inventor of the British Harrier "jump-jet" technology and I was a lowly Ops Analysis worker. It was kismet that we met and he took a shine to me. Besides teaching me the proper recipe for Mint Juleps, he was a print art connoisseur and an excellent literary critic, especially of film noir detective stories. Though he has passed from this earthy frame, I owe Gaz much for his advice for this effort. Thank you, buddy! I'll catch up with you on the other side of the veil.

To my fans and mystery readers everywhere. Thank you for reading this *homage* to Dashiell Hammett, Raymond Chandler, James Ellroy, F. Scott Fitzgerald, Roscoe Arbuckle, and Buster Keaton, who frolicked in the San Francisco Bay area at the tail end of the American Prohibition.

To Delphine Cingal, *Maître d' des conférences à l'Université de Paris II-Assas:* Thank you for being the first literary professional to "discover" me.

To Alexandria Constantinova Szeman, editor and publisher: You are my Szeman-Sensei. May all your dreams come true.

To the multi-talented actor John Hannah, who is also a marvelous photographer, for giving my publisher permission to use one of the photos of his lovely wife, actor Joanna Roth, as the cover art for this book. No other photo would have worked so well. Thank you for your gracious consent.

To John and Kayoko Barbour, the owners of Moss Beach Distillery, for your tremendous interest in my project, and your generous permission to use the vintage photographs as well as their contemporary counterparts.

To Melissa (Mel) Vega and Bev Anolin (of Moss Beach Distillery), and Robin Gotfrid (of Rogue Web Works LLC), for gathering all the photographs my publisher requested and getting copies of them to her. The photos helped me make Frank's Place come even more alive, and I value your participation in my research.

To the keepers of the Roscoe Arbuckle flame. Thanks for everything you do to keep the truth alive.

To Chris DeBlaey of Hoogerhyde Safe & Lock Inc., and to Guy Zani Jr. of the Antique Safe Collector, who were fabulous about answering my questions about vintage safes.

Table of Contents

*Author Photo, BIO, Amazon Page, Website,
Facebook, Twitter, Contact*

Roadhouse Affairs

Great tales spring from real truth,
but don't let little things like facts
get in the way of a good story.

Little Big Man,
Lakota survivor of the
Battle of the Little Bighorn

Chapter One

The morning quiet shattered. Outside on Main Street, a gun fired, big, like a Colt .45. I peered across the dance floor in the nearly empty bar toward the double door at the front and waited. The snapping sounds of .38s and .22s mixed with the big cannon, playing a crescendo in the street, before the .45 barked twice to finish the one-act gun play.

Everything was quiet. I counted to thirty. Whatever it was, it wasn't my problem. I dropped my hand from the Smith and Wesson .38 in my shoulder-holster and picked up my fork. Only five months left on my detective license. I'd have to work something out after that to legally carry my piece.

With alcohol, gambling, and prostitution forbidden in the states, but readily available six miles south of the border in Tijuana, Mexico, Hollywood's ascendant wealth fueled the growth of Tijuana's pleasure palaces. The nicest was the *Agua Caliente* Hotel with a Casino, horse racing track, and golf course. Next was the Mexicali Beer Hall with a polished oak bar that ran the length of the block-long building, where *cervezas*, whiskey, wine, and cocktails could be had any hour of the day. The Margarita drink and the Caesar salad were both invented in Tijuana, and their popularity grew with the town.

But like any big American city, the glitz was just a veneer covering layers of grit, grime, and crime. Tijuana was a mile of bars, each one pretending to be the only one on the strip with liquor and pretty girls. The harder they tried, the more they blended into a lumpy mish-mash of sun-faded buildings as textured as overcooked oatmeal. Dingy side streets provided hiding places for the gin joints too ashamed to show their *façades* on the main thoroughfare.

In the middle of the strip was a typical place distinguished only by a large gilded horseshoe over the doors. Inside on the right, an oak-topped bar ran half the length of the building with room for ten bartenders during racing season. The left wall was lined with one-armed bandits that stole change from patrons who lacked the will or skill to gyrate on the dance floor. In the evenings, a greasy little orchestra cranked out *win, place,* and *show* tunes from a raised platform. Beside the bandstand were rows of low-walled booths. In the last one, a hare-lipped man pulled pills from a keno game bag while a kid marked the board behind him for the few players to see. A poorly drawn but brightly painted bullfighter covered the wall opposite the bar. A metaphor for the town, what the artist lacked in talent he made up for in size.

It was December, and 1930 was fading into the past. A scrawny Christmas tree with too few branches and too much tinsel stood watch beside the front door. Greasy kitchen odors and the bar-back tang mingled with the smell of dirt roads and tobacco smoke from the dozen people who comprised the late morning crowd. A breeze stirred spider webs that spanned the transoms, trying to clear the air from the night before.

I sat in the front left booth, doing my best to chew what locals called a breakfast steak. It wasn't so bad after I taught the cook to beat it senseless with a hammer before letting the flames lick it. The flavor mingled well with the tall Black and White Scotch whisky for which I'd paid premium. The typical whiskey these bars poured was near poison, but at least it kept the water honest, most of the time.

My last trip to the Horseshoe was in 1927. A *chiquita* named Silvia had tried to get me to buy a flotilla of hooch on the first night. I bought just enough to acquire the moniker "Painless." Too bad for her, I was there to snatch her boyfriend, Dockside Freddy, who was living under the name of a man he had murdered. I made sure he swung for it.

But that was old news on stone tablets. The Depression broke out on Black Thursday, October 24, 1929. Thirteen months later, it was tough all over, but the soup kitchen lines were shorter in San Francisco than most other cities. The American Detective Agency had felt the pinch, too. With fewer cases, I did The Chief a favor and retired, giving him one less mouth to feed. The pension wasn't much, but it went a lot further in Mexico.

That's how I found myself chewing tough beef in TJ. Time had passed, even in old Mexico. Silvia had two children by her replacement boyfriend. A new bevy of babes conned patrons into buying extra drinks. I was fatter, and no longer hunted men, but they still called me "Painless."

The bar doors swung open, allowing a brief view of daylight to penetrate the dingy interior. Footsteps scuffed the wooden floor and stopped at the bar. I'd been off the clock for so long, I didn't care who it was. Even so, I made sure my rod was ready in my shoulder-holster. I pushed aside the finished *San Diego Union* crossword puzzle and set my teeth to chewing another bite.

After a minute, the man found a beer and his way to my table. He held the neck of his bottle between his thumb and index finger. The next finger had a knuckle wrapped in adhesive tape: the signal of an undercover detective hoping for a meeting. My hat hung on a hook next to my booth, prohibiting me from fixing an imaginary dent, the counter-sign to his taped finger. I gave him a nod instead.

Tradecraft satisfied, he sat down. I would have known that freckled face with happy gray eyes anywhere. He was the big-boned Irishman, Sean McGervey, from the Los Angeles office of the American Detective Agency. His broad shoulders nearly filled his side of the booth as he sat angled with his long legs sticking out the side and into the room.

I swallowed my bite and shooed away the *chiquita* who trailed him.

"It's business, Rosa. We'll call you when it's over."

I eyed McGervey.

"What happened out front?"

"No idea," he said, his face impassive.

"What brings you to Tijuana?"

"Chief asked me to find you."

"I'm all out of prizes."

He shrugged.

"I'm on the clock."

"What's the story?"

"He needs you back."

I drank some of my Scotch. McGervey pulled on his beer, his *Claddagh* ring clinking on the bottle.

"Forget it," I said. "I'm retired. I'm done with chasing crooks. I chase girls now."

He raised an eyebrow.

"They run slower here," I said.

"He told me to pester you until you called him."

Maybe my Chief hadn't read my retirement memorandum.

"So that's the price of submission?"

"Yours or mine?"

"Both."

I pushed my meal to the side, lit a Fatima, and levered my fat body onto my feet.

Catching the bartender's eye, I said, "I need to use the office, okay?"

"Hokay, *señor.*"

"Come on, McGervey. Let's go see what's up."

He followed me to the back where an ornate beaded curtain hid a hallway to a dilapidated office by the rear door. I sat behind the scratched mahogany desk and picked up the candlestick telephone. McGervey took the sturdy wooden chair next to the door.

I toggled the hook, blew into the mouthpiece, and brought the cone at the end of the wire to my ear. The operator came on the line.

"*Hola,*" I said in my best Spanish. "*Por favor,* San Francisco *en los Estados Unidos. Numero* West *uno tres seis dos, y invertia el costo. Gracias.*"

I hung the earpiece in its cradle and waited. McGervey crossed his legs. Detectives were used to waiting. I lit another Fatima off the old one.

I wondered what The Chief would want with me. With the Depression, there were plenty of men out looking for work. I wondered what McGervey knew, and what he was thinking.

The phone rang. I picked up the blower.

"*Sí?*"

"*Tengo listo su conexión.*"

"*Gracias, señora.*"

I waited.

The shopworn voice of The Chief — the American Detective Agency's San Francisco manager — came from the earpiece.

"How's your tan?"

"Not bad, but it's winter down here, too."

"Are you bored yet?"

The Chief knew me, all right: I was nothing without something to stand for.

"What's on the lot?"

"Alma Spreckels, widow of the sugar tycoon, has a situation. Her son, nineteen-year-old Adolph Jr., is being blackmailed for a wild night at Frank Torres' Roadhouse in Half Moon Bay. Mrs. Spreckels won't tolerate her status in the Social Register being compromised by scandal."

"Blackmail's a regular racket. You don't need me to run that down."

"It's tricky nowadays. With all the bank closings, the crooks are putting their money with the mob. The blackmail money goes to Genaro Broccolo in San Francisco, then…"

"Why's a gunsel like Broccolo running the mob's bank?"

I rubbed the side of my nose, quelling an itch.

"He's the *Capo* now. You remember Don Boca getting gunned down in July of '29?"

I grunted in agreement.

"Well, it took a while, but Broccolo took over. He's consolidated the rackets as far south as Redwood City. Like I said, he's now the bank for the local hoods. The blackmail money gets dropped at a North Beach book, and is transferred to Frank Torres, the ex-yegg who owns the Roadhouse in Half Moon Bay. We can't track who the money goes to after that."

"Frank Torres, eh? And you think my long-time acquaintance with Torres will let me sweet-talk it out of him?"

"While my operatives work on it regular," he said, his voice remaining flat, "you could set up shop at his Roadhouse and spot the blackmailers as they set up another mark."

I rubbed the back of my neck.

"Who're the other fish?"

"There are two more that we know of, but only Mrs. Spreckels is willing to pay to stop it. She doesn't mind if the others benefit when we clean out the whole rat's nest."

"What's your offer?"

"She's paying premium. I can bring you in as a contract stringer, undercover, of course."

That trumped learning to dance *La Cucaracha*. Maybe I could polish my armor and tilt at this windmill.

"Okay, I'm in, but I'll need some new suits."

I turned to McGervey.

"Let's get me back into the shooting game."

Chapter Two

The 1920s were a fine, wild time, and San Francisco had answered the call of the wild. Prohibition had separated people into the Wets and the Dries. The City was so wet, it dripped. The Depression was a slap in the face, but it didn't stop the party. Laugh and have another drink!

San Francisco ran on fun, and who knew fun better than Roscoe "Fatty" Arbuckle? Eight years earlier, after the petite Virginia Rappe had died during a three-day party held in Roscoe's hotel suite, William Randolph Hearst had convicted Hollywood's biggest comedy star of rape and murder in the pages of the *San Francisco Examiner*. It didn't matter that Roscoe was acquitted: his acting career was over. He took up directing under the name William B. Goodrich.

Tired of Hollywood's regular grind, he played Broadway in *Baby Mine*, then helped open Bimbo's — an espresso-paced club here in The City — using the interior of his own failed Culver City nightclub, giving it to Bimbo's for the cost of shipping. At night, in the hidden speakeasy, feather-festooned chorus girls danced to a jazz band while patrons drank gin from coffee cups, and Dolfina seemed to swim nude in a huge tank behind the bar. The chorus girls were probably still asleep during luncheon, but the dining room served a decent fare. The Chief was buying, and I was hungry.

I stepped off the Market Street car at Felton and bought a fresh rose for my lapel from a girl in the street curb flower booth while a handful of carolers sang.

> Good King Wenceslas looked out,
> on the Feast of Stephen,
> When the snow lay round about,
> deep and crisp and even;
> Brightly shone the moon that night,
> though the frost was cruel,

When a poor man came in sight,
gathering winter fuel.

I dropped my Fatima on the sidewalk and ground it out with my shoe. Shaking another from the pack almost emptied it. I bought fresh smokes from a newsie at a corner-stand full of men with large faces and pocket watches to match.

"Bring me flesh, and bring me wine,
bring me pine logs hither:
Thou and I shall see him dine,
when we bear them thither. "
Page and monarch, forth they went,
forth they went together;
Through the rude wind's wild lament
and the bitter weather.

While I had laid low in Mexico, my two favorite newspapers had merged to become the *Call Bulletin*. The masthead looked funny to me, but the headlines didn't. Hunters Point shipyard just laid off 8,000 workers, cutting down to one shift a day and a four-day work week.

The tough times seen everywhere else had finally arrived in The City. I lit my Fatima with a wood match, and then walked the half block to Bimbo's. A faint tang of brine wafted in from the bay.

The restaurant's arched windows were draped in pine bough garland, and a man dressed as Santa Claus gave candy canes to folks, opening the door for them to enter. I left my hat and overcoat with the cloakroom girl, and espied The Chief.

He sat at a table against the wall, halfway into the main dining area. He was as plump as when I last saw him, but he looked a half shade grayer, older than his actual seventy-two years, and the herd of white whiskers on his upper lip had thinned. His baby-pink grandfatherly face was tinged with ash, but his blue eyes were still as sharp as Guillotine's blade. His nicely pressed suit was tasteful while being utterly anonymous. A gentle smile displayed a politeness that went no deeper than the skin on which it hung, his compassion exhausted from fifty years of crook-hunting.

I dropped my fat body into a seat facing the street.

"I thought you'd be more tanned," he said. "You don't look much different than when you retired."

"I haven't fully converted to sun worship yet."

"That's good. I need an experienced man at the Roadhouse."

Our waiter arrived. The Chief ordered the special of pot roasted beef with vegetables and coffee for both of us.

"Why me?" I asked.

"You were a reliable detective before you retired. With all the Wobbly activity, headquarters pulled my best guys for strike-breaking squads."

Back in '29, busting the heads of union organizers from the Industrial Workers of the World for the industrialists who'd hired the Agency had been the straw that had broken my camel's back, and I'd quit.

"I don't want to take a job so somebody can be freed-up to attack Wobblies."

"It's not like that," he said. "I was already short-handed when this rich client showed up. I know you're still steamed at the Agency, but I'm desperate for experienced hands. I need you back on the job."

So I wasn't freeing anybody up for a fight.

"My opinion of the Agency hasn't changed, but I suppose I can stake out the Roadhouse for you."

"Here's what we have on the case, and some operating capital."

He passed me a brown paper portfolio tied with red string, and an envelope containing a banker's pack of C-notes.

"If you need more," he said, "let me know. I'll need your expense reports each month."

"Like usual. So, what can you tell me?"

"Not a thing. The money trail goes cold at the Roadhouse. The Spreckels' kid had his amusement there. It stands to reason you should be there watching."

"I'll take care of it."

"I renewed your detective license and had Josephine book you a room."

He took a leather card case from his inside coat pocket.

"And I had the printer make some cards for you."

I scowled. He gave me a few seconds of his blank expression.

"The cards say you're retired."

I rubbed my thumb along the side of my index finger.

"How antsy is the client?"

"She's a patient bird. She'll pay the blackmail for as long it takes, until we root out the whole problem. She doesn't want this cropping up again."

Our food arrived. We ate in silence.

A flurry of activity at the door got our attention. I looked and saw a woman nobody could forget. I sure hadn't. I'd been a rookie working skip-traces in Illinois. She'd been breaking in as a dancer. The Agency had pulled me out just as we'd been getting close. That was when I was young and thin, when she was unknown.

Since then, Loie Fuller had set tongues to wagging on both sides of the Atlantic by performing her notorious "Serpentine Dance" in Paris at the *Folies-Bergère*. Her lithe form in flowing chiffon became the image of *la Belle Époque,* known on this side of the pond as the Art Nouveau period. That dream ended with a bang: a Vasić hand grenade, small arms fire, and the Archduke Franz Ferdinand's assassination. The Great War wasn't so great. Yet, here was Loie, tempting me to dream again.

She passed our table without noticing me. We both had gray hair, and added padding, but hers was in all the right places. The lady with her was formidable — six-feet-tall in a long gown — her square shoulders suggesting a working class lineage. She carried herself like a battleship at sea. They took the table in the center of the room while the *maître d'* followed in their wake.

The Chief used an eyebrow to indicate the two women.

"That's Mrs. Spreckels, and her friend… "

"Loie Fuller."

A sigh escaped my lips.

"The crack in your *façade*'s leaking air."

Sarcasm was the only emotion he had left.

"I used to know her when we were young and reckless."

"Lucky you."

We offered a moment of silence for dead dreams and missed opportunities. Then he told their story.

"Mrs. Alma Spreckels met *La Loie* in Paris, and the two became fast friends. The Spreckels widow was rolling in dough but lacked social contacts. The dancer knew everyone who was anybody but was often short on cash. Alma and Loie used each other, as famous friends do."

"Lucky them."

I thumb-rubbed the itch that started in my index finger.

"Mrs. Spreckels is one of the biggest art collectors in America. She imported thirteen Rodin masterworks."

"If she can afford French sculptures, she can afford us," I said.

"That's why we're having lunch. She wanted to see you. I told her that it would have to be like this, so that nobody would connect you to the blackmail of her son."

At least I had on a new suit for the occasion.

"She can look all she wants," I said.

Mrs. Spreckels said something to Loie, who looked at me with an appraising eye. It took a minute before her eyes opened wide. She smiled.

I winked, and then smoothed my right eyebrow.

She turned and said something to Mrs. Spreckels. A short conversation ended with the client looking at The Chief. She gave a curt nod.

"You're approved," he said.

"I got that."

Our waiter appeared.

"Any dessert today?"

I looked at The Chief.

He looked at me.

"Impress our client. Skip the pie and go to work."

That was okay by me. Seeing Loie made my gut feel like it had already left the room. I stood. The Chief's smile might have meant anything. He ordered apple pie as I left.

Since I'd need more freedom than riding the train could give me, and since the rich client was footing the bill, I hired a swanky gray Ford-A Tudor Sedan. I drove south to Frank Torres' Roadhouse, wondering if I still had what it took to fight crime all by myself.

Chapter Three

B ayshore Drive hugs the scrub-brush-covered coast from San Francisco to Monterey. On the north end of Half Moon Bay, it skirts an isolated bluff that overlooks Moss Beach. There, off Marine Boulevard, on Beach Way, Frank Torres had given up the life of a safe-cracking yegg to open his Roadhouse. Frank knew the perfect location to start his bootlegging operation, and Moss Beach was it.

A huge sign signaled the turn to Frank's Place, promising "Dancing," "Good Things to Eat," and "A Restful Place to Stay." I didn't know how those who'd been blackmailed felt about the "restful" part. I pulled into a circular white gravel drive that connected Bayshore to the rows of covered carports where patrons could stow their cars out of the frequent coastal drizzle. Flowerbeds and ornate shrubbery flanked the car lot and outlined the club.

Frank's was a large rectangular building, built of chalky white stone. Next door, the slate-blue asbestos shingle siding of the two-story Marine View Hotel stretched north along the bluff. An enclosed breezeway connected the two buildings. Depending on the season and time of day, swirling mists added a sense of mystery and romance that some folks found as attractive as the Pacific Ocean view.

Rumors were that Torres had picked the site because the bluff sat atop a sea cave, and he had tunneled into it, gaining access to the beach below. After multiple raids failed to find any sea cave access, the District Attorney and the San Mateo County Sheriff had given up searching.

But with the amount of Canadian liquor that Pacific Ocean smugglers were running through Torres' place, that access had to be somewhere. Thirsty customers up and down the central California corridor made his Roadhouse the coast's most successful speakeasy, thus also creating the perfect breeding ground for all manner of pikers and pills, all looking to pull off some big caper — including blackmail.

I parked the Ford-A Tudor in front of the hotel. The Roadhouse was starting the swing-shift party, the opening act for the night's festivities. Christmas was still weeks away, but they already had enough holly and ivy decorating the lobby to tempt even Santa to visit this tough hole.

At one side of the main staircase, a towering Douglas Fir filled the lobby with its fragrant scent. All its ornaments were silver and gold, even the snowmen, angels, elves, reindeer, and Santas. Strands of silver beads glimmered like exotic pearls encircling its long green body. Points of white glowed from the center of tear-shaped, mercury-glass lights strung among the branches. I hadn't seen anything like that down in TJ.

I tossed the car keys to the attendant and walked to the front desk. All the male employees sported red-and-green plaid bowties, threaded with silver and gold. They looked like wrapped presents under the tree. I gave the clerk my name.

"Your travel bureau called."

He signaled the concierge, and then focused on me.

"You're expected. Mr. Torres will be here momentarily."

"I'd like a room on the top floor, on the end near the nightclub."

"Mr. Torres selected a suite for you in the middle. It's quite nice."

"I'm sure it is, but unless he's paying for it, I want a room on the nightclub end. And have the kitchen send up a pot of coffee and a sandwich."

The clerk nodded and exchanged the keys.

"Here you are, sir, Room 228."

He looked over my shoulder.

"Mr. Torres is here."

I turned. The door to the breezeway connecting the hotel and the club clicked shut as Frank Torres crossed the lobby. He wasn't wearing the requisite holiday bowtie. Above his broad shoulders, his long face, brown eyes, and thick black eyebrows showed no expression: a horse-face if ever I saw one. His mouth almost smiled as he held out his mitt for a shake.

"Look at you," he said. "I thought you were dead."

"I paid some guys to spread that around. It's a useful rumor for a flatfoot looking to retire."

His eyes narrowed. He stepped close.

"What do you want at my Roadhouse?"

"I got homesick. Maybe a month in the old stomping grounds will be the cure."

His nostrils flared.

"Are you sure you aren't here to stir up trouble?"

I hung a facsimile of sincerity on my face.

"I'm here for the scenery. Carmel is supposed to be lovely. I've never seen it, nor Monterey at less than car speed."

He tilted his head forward and cocked an eyebrow.

"You're not going to shoot me again, are you?"

"It just grazed your side. You know I was trying to stop the girl with the gray eyes from escaping with her dandy. Besides, I'm retired now."

Torres was uncertain what to make of me, but I was a paying customer. That was probably good enough for him, as long as his boys kept an eye on me.

"Well, okay, but no bothering the plungers. I need them to gamble at my tables."

"I wouldn't have it any other way."

I gave him a grin.

"This is such a nice place. What's it take to get the nickel tour?"

"You already know where my office and private quarters are."

"Yes, but I want to see the whole shebang, now that I'm staying here."

"I'll think about it. In the meantime, please enjoy yourself. If you need something special, just ask."

He made a gesture to the clerk, and then turned toward the stairs and his second-floor suite.

I stood there a few more seconds. In the distance I could hear the tune of "O Little Town of Bethlehem" on a piano. The desk clerk pretended to clear his throat.

I looked at him. He placed a French postcard in my hand. On the front was a woman with her skirt hiked up, fiddling with her hosiery. Despite the season, she wasn't standing under any mistletoe. On the back something was printed in fancy script:

Special Introductory Offer:
Two for the Price of One.

"What's this?" I asked.

"You appear to be a man of discretion."

I waited, card in hand. He lowered his voice slightly.

"The coupon can be redeemed with any of the ladies at the other end of the second floor from your room."

I pocketed the card, thinking of how the young sugar tycoon may have been taken in by just such an offer.

"How nice. Since you're so accommodating, send up a bottle of Rye and a siphon of soda water."

A pair of black-suited goons looked out of a doorway, giving me the evil eye. They weren't dressed in any holiday finery. I hoped that they weren't looking for trouble on my first day back at work.

Chapter Four

M y hotel room was just off the stairwell next to the Roadhouse entrance. The side window afforded a good view of the front door. That left the highway side and rear exits uncovered. The last time I'd been here, those exits weren't accessible by the public.

A maid of average height, with narrow shoulders and flared hips, was still at work on my room when I walked through the open door. Her uniform was so formal that she could have been mistaken for a nurse. Her raven hair was close-bobbed, like a flapper. It was out of style, but looked good on her. Her pert breasts rode high, the way fashion magazines preferred, but she was too far away from the runways of Paris to have been noticed, even with the sprig of holly peeking over the top of her polished silver name-tag.

"I'm sorry sir," she said, her pale skin reddening. "I'll just be a moment."

Her makeup almost hid the late-healing stage of a black eye.

"Pay me no mind."

I walked through the sitting room, the dressing room with a bathroom to the left, and entered the bedroom. My bag was open on the table between the wardrobe and the matching dresser. I slipped off my double-breasted suit-coat, and hung it on the oak Gentleman's valet. The window facing the Roadhouse was raised, drawing air from the open rear window that overlooked the bluff and the ocean below. The sound of surf churning on the rocky coast was distant. A smell of fish mixed with brine and kelp carried on the breeze.

I returned to the sitting room and hung my Fedora on the Bentwood coat-tree by the door. Still wearing my vest over my shirt, I sat down. I snuffed my Fatima in the ashtray and lit another, sending a lungful of smoke to ride the breeze out the open door. I enjoyed the view while the maid finished dusting. She went to the door and peeked outside before going to her cart, quickly returning with bed linens. She scanned the parking lot as she cleared the door, looking relieved to be back inside as she disappeared into the rear rooms.

A bellhop appeared with a tray and set it on the table in front of me, deftly sliding the potted Poinsettia aside. He poured coffee from a large silver carafe into a Delft china cup with saucer, and then removed the linen cloth that covered a nicely stacked ham and cheese sandwich on pumpernickel. Dill pickle spears and a pile of *crudités* filled the rest of the plate. An icing-covered sugar cookie in the shape of a snowman rested on a small plate that matched the other hand-painted blue china. The fifty-cent room-service bill was pricey, but it was a resort hotel, and the client had the jack to pay the freight. I signed the chit and pulled a dime from my pocket for a tip. Over his red-and-green plaid bow-tie, the boy smiled and left.

I tucked the ivory linen napkin under my chin, over my collar and tie, and took a bite of the sandwich. My Fatima smoldered in the ashtray. A dash of horseradish in the dark brown mustard went well with the hickory smoked ham and sharp Irish cheddar. I left the pitcher of cream untouched as I drank some of the dark, strong java. I could get to like this kind of stake-out. It sure beat cold nights shivering in the rain outside a flophouse.

Between furtive glances toward the open door, the maid finished making the bed.

"What's eating you, Sister?"

A startled look, like a rabbit in a hawk's shadow, crossed her face. She blushed again.

"Whatever do you mean, sir?"

"You act like the rides in the parking lot are going to bite you."

"I just don't want to be seen, that's all."

She smoothed her unwrinkled apron.

"Who are you afraid of?"

"I don't want to get in trouble."

"Not with me."

I dug for my wallet.

"I'm a detective."

I gave her my card.

"Like Race Williams in *Black Mask* magazine?"

I suppressed a grimace.

"Sort of."

She ran her left index finger across my card, taking her time reading my name, and then looked up.

"It says you're retired."

I showed her my gun in its shoulder-holster.

"I can still settle somebody's hash."

She slipped my card into a hidden pocket, and wrung a pair of hands that seemed too small for her long arms and torso. Brushing her still unwrinkled apron, she looked up, searching my face.

I let her get what she could from my brown eyes. She must have found something she liked because she sat in the chair next to me, her hands clasped in her lap.

"What's your name?"

"Elizabeth Claire Donovan."

I looked at her name-tag, its narrow silver band too small to hold that many letters.

"People call me Cayte," she said.

"What's got you so jumpy, Cayte?"

"I'm afraid he'll find me."

Her slender frame shook as tears crawled down her cheeks.

"Who?"

"My husband."

This sort of thing was never good; there were agency directives against getting involved in domestic squabbles. She didn't seem to have a grifter's touch: she probably had a *bona fide* problem. Lately, the world seemed full of them.

I waited.

She continued.

"We moved here from Iowa, looking for a better chance. When he couldn't find steady work, he started drinking."

She pulled a cotton handkerchief from her apron and dabbed her eyes.

"He beats me."

She turned away.

I took her hand, put it flat on her knee, and then patted it.

"I feel sick about leaving little Jack," she said. "He's only four, but I couldn't take another beating."

With her moist, imploring eyes, she looked like an angel in a *de Riquer* painting.

"I took a cab as far as my money would go. It dropped me here. John Contina, Mr. Torres' nephew who plays piano in the club, saw me crying on the steps. He got me this job. He introduced me to Anna. She works here, and she lets me stay with her. I pay rent and for my own food and everything. I'm hoping to get my own place after New Year's."

"Your secret's safe with me," I said.

She took my hand.

"Thank you for understanding."

I understood that her man was a louse. No woman needed that, not even the ones I'd arranged to have locked away from the public. There are ways to break a man's hands so he can never fight again.

I needed an informant, and this maid would fit the bill. I lit another Fatima.

"If you see your husband, let me know. I'll fix it so he won't bother you anymore."

"But I couldn't afford to hire…"

"On the house."

"Thank you! Oh, thank you!"

"Now, go fix your face so you look okay when you finish here."

I glanced at my sandwich. One bite gone, but now so was my appetite. I drank the java and poured another cup. I stared at the bright red Poinsettia a moment or two.

I had only her side of the story. Sure, her shiner told a violent tale, but that wasn't enough to give her *Carte Blanche*. She could be a gold-digger with her own spin on the story to sell.

There was a tap on the door. Another bellhop stood there, older than the first one, but also wearing the festive holiday bow-tie, holding a basket covered in a cloth.

"You read my mind."

I motioned him in. Through the open door, the chorus of "God Rest Ye Merry Gentlemen" could be heard coming from the piano downstairs.

The bellhop placed the basket on the other chair, and unloaded an ice bucket, a soda water siphon, a fifth of Canadian Rye, and two highball glasses.

My mouth watered. I rubbed my chin. The room service bill said *caviar and crackers, $5*. I signed it and gave him four bits from my pocket. He, too, smiled and left.

I pushed the cold coffee away, took the napkin from under my chin and covered the sandwich plate, saving it for later. I put a cube of ice in a highball glass, poured three fingers of Rye whiskey, and filled the glass from the siphon. I took a long slow drink that drained half the glass, enjoying the crisp medicinal smell and the pale amber color.

I turned toward the maid, who had just emerged from the bathroom.

"All done?" I asked.

"Yes."

Her fresh coat of face paint all but concealed the mottled green and blue skin around her left eye. She looked at me with entreating eyes.

"You won't say anything to Mr. Torres, will you?"

"I'm not the kind to kiss and tell."

She blushed almost as red as the berries in the sprig of holly which graced her name-tag before she left, closing the door behind her.

She didn't seem the type to try and play me, but as a woman, she could learn that trade quick. On the other hand, she could become an informant. I'd have to play my cards right to get the most from what I was dealt. Maybe I could see about sneaking a few cards from the bottom of the deck.

I drained my glass and fixed another. I undid my vest and tie, removed them, went to the bedroom, and put them on the oak valet with my suit jacket. I opened the valet drawer and put in my wallet, watch, tie-pin, and ring. I closed the bedroom's side window and curtains, and then unpacked my luggage.

Lifting the leather bag, I turned it upside down and pressed the two recessed buttons on either side of the bottom plate. The clasps rotated and the bottom rose a bit, allowing me to lift it free. I checked the envelope of cash before taking The Chief's brown portfolio back to the table.

Chapter Five

The hatcheck girl said nothing as she passed me my ticket over the walnut counter decorated with holly. She was cute enough to be the bait in a blackmail gambit, but not outgoing enough for a recruiter. She smiled at the tip I left.

I squared my black bow-tie and tugged at the white shirt cuffs inside the sleeves of my dull black dinner jacket. It was fashionable enough without being the height of fashion: if I had to lurk in any dark corners or tail a suspect, shiny lapels just wouldn't do.

The 'shine pointed at my shoes. I sat for a treatment. He gripped a tin of black Shinola-Bixby in his left hand, a stumpy middle finger missing its tip showed over the rim. The pale skin around his wedding band was tinted green, but it wasn't in honor of the season.

"Is that the new shoe polish?" I asked.

"Yeah, you use less of it, but get a higher shine."

He touched the polish with his brush and set to work. Looking up, he gave me a slit-eyed grin.

"I've got the Win-and-Place for tomorrow's third race at Aqueduct."

"That's dandy," I said.

"Really, mister! If we can figure out the Show, we'll have the Trifecta."

"That may be tough; they're running on the inner track, now. Dirt's hard to figure, given New York's weather and how different horses do in mud."

"I knew you were a wise-head, soon as I seen you. I've got the horses, and you've got the angles, see? So let's compare notes and place a bet."

That yarn was old before I was young.

"I don't play the bangtails."

He gave me a bug-eyed stare.

"Your loss, mister, 'cause it's a sure thing."

"Of that, I'm certain."

I was also certain that the shoeshine, though he was definitely a schemer, lacked the brains to run a blackmail racket.

I paid for the shine, and then crossed the festive lobby to the lectern at the entrance of the supper club.

"Good evening."

The red-headed hostess' slender form made her appear taller than her five-foot five-inch height; her average curves seemed statuesque on her compact frame. Her long neck finished in an almond-shaped face with wide-set green eyes, full lips, and a nose that just missed being upturned. She wore a long-sleeved black dress, hemmed so it grazed her well-turned ankles. Her requisite sprig of decorative holly was tucked behind her right ear. She raised the pen in her long-fingered hand.

"Would you like a table for the evening?"

"Yes, but just for supper. I hope to mingle after that."

"Your waiter can answer any questions about our entertainment possibilities. Will anyone else be joining you this evening?"

"No, but perhaps I'll meet someone later."

"You just might."

She winked and then made a few marks on the sheet in front of her. She couldn't be serious, flirting with this fat old man; she must just play it cute for all the single marks that came her way. Maybe she *was* trolling for a blackmail target.

"Please follow me," she said, taking a black fabric-covered menu from a recessed shelf.

As she led me into the club, the rear view was just as nice. An oval opening in her dress exposed her back, as pale as moonlight. California's Bay Area fogs are no help in getting a little color into your skin. Maybe she'd like to share some Mexican sunshine with me?

And maybe I had a chance of getting ice in hell when I got there, too.

Three chandeliers and innumerable wall sconces cast a warm orange glow on the hardwood dance floor, flanked on each side by two rows of tables, each with Poinsettias in silver or gold pots in the center. Columns separated the ballroom from carpeted aisles that ran the perimeter of the building. I knew from previous Roadhouse visits that the back stairs on the inland side led to Torres' living quarters on the second floor of the club.

Above the wainscoting, windows lined the wall facing the ocean-side cliff. Fringed valances stretched across the tops of each window while, at the wooden frames between them, the drapes were pulled together and yoked with a braided gold rope that matched the valance fringe. Every twenty feet, French doors offered access to the terrace outside that overlooked the beach and the ocean. The cloud bank on the horizon prevented the setting sun from shining through.

A square-shouldered young man of medium build with wavy black hair played a Steinway Baby Grand beside the dance floor.

> The holly bears a berry
> As red as any blood,
> And Mary bore sweet Jesus Christ
> To do poor sinners good.

The placard on the easel read *John Contina*, the young man Cayte had mentioned. Frank Torres' nephew. Being a relative must have liberated him from the obligatory red-and-green bow-tie. Still, anyone who worked here was a suspect in the blackmail scheme. My antennae were out.

> The holly bears a prickle
> As sharp as any thorn,
> And Mary bore sweet Jesus Christ
> On Christmas Day in the morn.

A band was setting up on a raised stage at the end of the dance floor while Contina continued playing traditional Christmas songs.

> The holly and the ivy
> Now are both well grown;
> Of all the trees that are in the wood
> The holly bears the crown.

Kid Ory's Creole Orchestra was emblazoned on the boxed music stands of the band on the raised stage. My acquaintance with Kid Ory started in the early 1920s when he headlined Oakland's Creole Cafe. He played most of San Francisco's hot spots and ritzy parties before he left for Chicago in '25.

24

At the Baby Grand, Contina segued from "The Holly and the Ivy" into "Angels We Have Heard on High." The hostess led me to a table on the inland side of the building. A few people watched the ocean from the terrace. One gestured wildly, turning to her companion.

I pointed with my chin.

"What's up on the veranda?"

The hostess looked.

"The whales are migrating south to Baja for the winter. They must have seen a spout."

"I'd like to see one, someday."

Her green eyes sparkled with mischief.

"Maybe I can show you a good spot to watch them?"

"That would be nice."

I smiled as she returned to the hostess station. I wondered how big a tip I would need to get the guided tour.

A waiter arrived, and I ordered the night's special of chicken consommé, artichoke-and-tomato salad, locally bagged grouse, potatoes, corn, string beans, and sliced avocado, with a finish of orange ice. A decade of Prohibition had killed the wine industry. Despite the dangers and criminal elements inherent in the illicit liquor trade, it was easier and less expensive to get a bottle of hard hooch than a mediocre bottle of wine. I ordered coffee with my meal.

Contina switched from traditional Christmas tunes to popular ones. He finished playing Fats Waller's "Ain't Misbehavin'," and launched into "I May Be Wrong, but I Think You're Wonderful." For an owner's nephew, he wasn't half bad. Maybe he could make it on the circuit if he tried.

And maybe he was clipping the clientele to finance a road-tour.

Barely a third of the tables were full, but twilight was still an hour away as we early-birds took our supper. Most tables were occupied by groups of couples in evening wear. Men with hair plastered flat to their heads sat beside women in glad rags who wore finger-waved or curling-iron hairstyles and makeup by Max Factor, or some knockoff brand. The women's hats were smaller this year, with shorter rims, and worn tilted to the side. Quite a few of the women wore no hats at all, and they had their hair done Greta Garbo style: side-parted with the wind-blown look, longer than the Clara Bow flapper length. Neither look had made it down to the *chiquitas* I was used to in Tijuana. White arms, shoulders, and collar-bones emerged from bright-colored gowns that also revealed bare backs. The hemlines were longer than when I'd left, but the gams were still fine. Jewelry sparked in the dimming light as they sat bracketed by men in dark dinner jackets, tuxes, and bow-ties.

Several men wearing workday suits sat at two tables in the rear. The armpit bulges under their coats were barely noticeable as they ate without conversation. They must be some of Torres' trouble boys having a repast before going on night shift. I examined them unobtrusively as I turned slightly in my chair, my arm on the back, pretending to gaze out at the ocean waves.

When my soup and salad dishes had been cleared, I got up and wandered toward the bandstand. Edward "Kid" Ory was the best trombone player I'd heard, and I listened to them all. After moving to Chicago, he became famous, working with the greats, like Louis Armstrong, Jelly Roll Morton, and King Oliver.

Kid saw me and stepped off the dais.

"Look at you!"

He grabbed my hand and shook it.

"I thought I'd seen a ghost, but it was only pale, pudgy you."

"It's good to see you, too, Edward. I thought you were in Chicago."

I shook a Fatima from my pack.

"I was, but this Depression hit hard there. It was bad: too few jobs for too many musicians. I came back to play a few gigs with the guys I cut records with. Then I'm dropping out. My brother's got a chicken ranch outside Los Angeles. I'm going to help him run it."

He gave me a light off his smoke.

I took a deep drag.

"Sounds like me. I retired, but came back for a visit."

I lifted my chin.

"How long's this gig last?"

"Through New Year's Eve."

He took a drag and popped a smoke ring before shooting a thin plume of smoke through it.

"You coming back through on your way south?" I asked.

"Yeah, we're here again in mid-January."

"If I'm still here, I'll stop by."

"You still owe me a bottle."

"It was a crooked deck," I objected. "But I'll have a bottle sent to the dressing room for old times' sake."

I started to leave, but turned back.

"What do you think about the piano player?"

"Contina? He's got a good touch and plays some fine stride piano. I offered to take him to Chicago, but he turned me down. He's a good musician, but it's not his main gig. Why?"

"Just making conversation," I said.

We flicked our ashes onto a passing busboy's tray.

"Well, I have to get set for the show."

He turned to the bandstand.

I returned to my table as the waiter brought the main course. While I ate, I observed the room. Long ago, I gave up trying to guess what kind of lives lurked behind the *façades* that people wore in public. Folks usually fell into one of two categories: citizens or suspects. That sounded too much like The Chief, but it was all I had left after decades on the job.

The crowd of suspects at the two rear tables stood to leave without paying their tab or having dessert. Two of them conversed while the others left the club. The one facing me pointed in my direction. The other one turned to look.

It was "Spider" Aures, and he'd recognized me.

Chapter Six

I had arranged Spider's last trip to the state penitentiary. His eyes narrowed and his mouth became a thin hard line. He turned his back to me, but his body didn't block my view enough to prevent me from seeing him draw his index finger across his throat. He and a few hundred other punks felt that way about me.

The one facing me nodded his head. Aures must have said something else, because his buddy nodded again. Aures put his hand on the other man's arm and turned him toward the door. They left without looking my way again.

On their way out, they passed a big man entering the room wearing a more-than-ample raincoat, even for his large frame. It wasn't until he pulled the oversized floppy hat from his head that I recognized "The Prince of Whales," Roscoe Arbuckle. He scanned the room before moving to the table next to mine. The hostess scurried after him. Despite his nearly 300 pounds, he moved with grace. A murmur started in the room, with people gesturing at the new arrival.

Dropping his rain-gear on a chair and sitting facing the entrance, he took the menu from the hostess and laid it on the table. When his waiter arrived, his watch on the door was steady, even as he answered the waiter's query with an excellent tenor voice.

"Just coffee for now."

The waiter gestured, and a busboy came to take Arbuckle's coat and hat.

I signaled the waiter before he could disappear.

"I need a bottle of Rye delivered to the band's dressing room, and what kind of booze can I get here, at the table?"

"I can bring you a pre-mixed gin and tonic or a martini."

"Can I get a pitcher of G&Ts?"

"I'll bring a full carafe."

"And five glasses," I added.

"And a bucket of ice," he said before leaving on his errand of mercy.

I had finished my supper but was still working on the coffee when the waiter arrived with the liquor.

"Follow me."

I stood and went to Arbuckle's table.

His round face turned to me, blue eyes sparkling.

"Yes?"

I gestured to the waiter's tray.

"Can I buy you a drink?"

"Thank you."

He smiled and gestured to the vacant chairs around his table.

"Please, join me."

His slight southern accent added charm to his words.

As the waiter unloaded the tray, I sat, leaving an empty seat between us. The waiter poured two drinks and departed.

Arbuckle raised his glass and smiled.

"Cheers!"

I returned the salute. We drank.

"Thank you, Mister..."

"My name's not important. I just wanted to tell you that folks don't believe everything they read in the newspapers."

His grin had the wattage of a Broadway marquee and of the Christmas tree in the lobby, combined.

"It's nice to hear that I still have fans."

I nodded.

"Droves."

"Wonderful. Then you'll like my news. Tonight I'm meeting a friend who's working behind the scenes on my comeback. I might get a new film contract."

"Let's hope it's not just a trip for biscuits, that there's some meat, too. Folks need some good news, nowadays. Seeing you back in films would ease our depression."

"You're most kind, sir."

His eyes narrowed.

"But I fear you have me at a disadvantage, sir."

"I'm a retired detective."

I gave him a card that he read and slipped into a vest pocket.

"I'm just taking a little holiday before I go native in Mexico."

"I hope you enjoy your well-earned retirement. I'm too young for that. I'm going to give it another shot."

At forty-three, he should take another poke at The Fates. My decades of scrubbing urban grime from the cityscape had left me more like The Chief than I liked. I had no dreams left of a better world nor any illusions that I made a difference. Sure, I'd put some crooks in jail, but in the big scheme of things, it didn't amount to a hill of beans.

I refilled our empty glasses, and then stood.

"You're expecting guests. I'll breeze, but leave you the eel juice."

"You don't need..."

I cut him off.

"Just a little 'thank you' for all you've done, and a little medicine for what you're still going through."

He smiled.

"I choose not to be defined by those events."

He was what I'd heard: a class act. After William Randolph Hearst's newspaper had turned Virginia Rappe's death into a scandal, Arbuckle lost his million-dollar acting contract. Some men have killed for less. Arbuckle became a director at Paramount, where he cast Marion Davies — Hearst's girlfriend — in major films. If that was what Arbuckle called "revenge," I guess I could stomach it.

I raised my glass to him, took a drink, and returned to my table. He resumed his watch on the door.

My waiter brought the orange ice. I asked for the check.

The hostess led a party of three into the room. A beaming Buster Keaton said something to the hostess; her laughter tinkled like holiday bells. Two others trailed, a man and a woman, both young; the male paid hopeful attention to the girl, while she paid more attention to the decor than to where she went, twice bumping into chairs as they moved to Arbuckle's table. As they came closer I recognized the young ones from recent Hollywood advertising promotions.

The film star and his guests were not my concern, but blackmailers are drawn to money, and people who worked in Hollywood were lousy with it. If a blackmailer was using the Roadhouse to pick his marks, he was bound to cozy up to them.

Despite his girth, Arbuckle's five-foot-ten-inch frame seemed to float to his feet when Buster Keaton entered the room.

"Bus!" he said, advancing to meet them.

"You look swell, Chief."

Keaton shook Arbuckle's hand, and grasped his arm above the elbow. Keaton, with dark hair and a square jaw, looked his thirty-five years. He was my height, five inches shorter than Arbuckle.

Keaton turned to the two he had brought to the party.

"These are my friends, Anita Page and Bob Montgomery. They're helping me make *Free and Easy*. It's a talkie."

"How nice. I'll have to make one of those, eventually."

Miss Page was a stunning waif, a few inches over five feet, in a flowing indigo dress that showed lovely lower legs and high-heeled pumps. Despite fourteen films in five years, the twenty-year-old actress still had an aura of innocence about her. I felt the full effect when she turned her blonde head and focused her over-sized blue eyes on me.

Robert Montgomery was tall, about six foot two. He was built like a footballer, but moved like a dancer. Last week, *Variety* had run an article about him, saying he was a promising twenty-four-year-old newcomer. His chiseled features and dark, wavy hair would sell a lot of tickets at the box office.

Arbuckle exchanged pleasantries with them and ushered them into seats.

The hostess returned to her post, while a waiter hovered in the distance.

Miss Page sat next to Keaton, who sat opposite Arbuckle at their six-place table. Montgomery sat on the other side of Page, murmuring into her ear. Arbuckle poured and passed the drinks.

They kept their voices low, but I was a professional eavesdropper. Contina had stopped playing and was fiddling with sheet music, one ear cocked toward the conversation. I picked up the weighty silver teaspoon and pulled the delicate bowl heaped with orange ice toward me. While I enjoyed the view of the beach and the ocean waves, I listened to the two stars.

Keaton focused on Arbuckle.

"It's good to have you back from New York. I thought you would do a few more years on Broadway."

"I might have, but Educational Studios asked me to direct a few pictures for them."

"They're in Burbank. What are you doing up here?"

"I got lucky. The owners of Bimbo's in San Francisco bought the interior from my Plantation Club that failed last year. I just finished overseeing the installation, and came down to the Roadhouse to have a little fun before studio work captures me. Thanks for meeting me here."

"It's a pleasure."

He looked at Page who was busy avoiding Montgomery's attempts to woo her.

"We had a break in production, and I thought they could use a change of scenery."

He returned his attention to Arbuckle.

"I needed a break from Natalie, and having these two with me blunts her suspicions."

Arbuckle leaned closer to Keaton.

"How bad is it?"

"She's hired a divorce lawyer."

Arbuckle patted Keaton's arm and sat back. Montgomery and Page didn't seem to notice.

"Did you hear that Bambina Delmont died?" Keaton asked.

"No, I hadn't. I don't like to speak ill of the dead, but she can rot in hell for the lies she spread about me after I refused her blackmail demand. Her other victims will be glad for the news."

He broke one of the smaller white roses away from the table centerpiece, and placed it in his buttonhole. When he noticed Miss Page looking at him, he pinched off a branch of holly with its red berries that was in amongst the white roses, and tucked it behind her right ear. She smiled at him. He was classy, all right. I feared Montgomery, despite his pretty hair and classic looks, didn't stand a chance with the girl.

"With Bambina's loud mouth shut for good," Keaton continued during the flower ceremony, "I can get started on your comeback. Here's the idea: next year, on the tenth anniversary of the scandal, we get *Motion Picture Magazine* to print an article, something like, Doesn't Fatty Arbuckle Deserve a Break? We get a lot of big names to sign on. The goal is to get the fans to demand your return to the screen."

"You think it will work?"

"I do."

Keaton smiled.

Their waiter approached and took their orders. I continued to work on my orange ice, turning, between bites, around in my chair toward the opposite side, to view the ocean cliff better.

Miss Page leaned forward to smell the Douglas Fir garland, studded with red berries and wrapped around the base of the floral centerpiece. Montgomery fiddled with the silver napkin holder around the napkin at the empty place next to him while Arbuckle took a drink.

"I wonder if you would help out a kid with a few introductions around town," said Arbuckle as Keaton sipped his own G&T. "Bob Hope. A few years ago, in Cleveland, he opened for me... great timing. He contacted me, and asked if I could help him get into Hollywood."

"Starting out is tough."

"Starting over again is tough."

Both looked wistful for a few moments as Arbuckle lifted the pitcher to refill everyone's glasses. Miss Page's was halfway full: she shook her head. Montgomery held his martini glass up for it to be filled. Arbuckle put the slightly sweating pitcher down between the centerpiece and the crystal candlestick with its silver candle.

"I'll see what I can do for your Bob Hope," Keaton said before he cocked his head. "You can do one for me. You know the act, The Three Stooges?"

It was Arbuckle's turn to nod as Montgomery bent his head closer to Miss Page's over the menu, pointing to something. She slid her own finger to another selection. I took the last bite of my orange ice and put the spoon down.

"Shemp Howard wants a shot at a dramatic role," said Keaton. "My deal at MGM is a little shaky. Maybe you can use him. The next time you're in town, meet with him, okay?"

"I will. Now let's see about some food before the night's festivities."

Arbuckle gestured, and their waiter appeared. After some discussion and more pointing at menus, the waiter gathered everyone's order and moved off. Miss Page and Montgomery put their napkins in their laps as they talked to each other, turning their bodies to involve Arbuckle and Keaton in the conversation. It soon became a topping-tournament of Hollywood insider news, each story stacked higher than the previous, about the inhabitants of the town constructed from ego. I'd already had my weekly ration of that from *Variety*. I didn't need a second dose.

I wrote my room number and signed the check, leaving enough to make the waiter happy, but not enough for me to develop a reputation as a butter-and-egg man with a big bankroll.

Chapter Seven

I made my way back to the reception area, near the breezeway that connected the club to the hotel. Two couples came in from the car lot, dressed in evening clothes. One woman wore a festive wrist-corsage with silver bells against a bed of white ribbons and rosebuds. The other wore pearl bracelets. A young man stopped leaning against the wall next to the cloakroom and walked toward the couples. He bumped into one of the men, both of whom were paying more attention to the women than to their surroundings. The young man was good, but he didn't completely hide his right hand as it moved the billfold into his own jacket. The group continued inside while the pickpocket stepped outside.

I moved to where I could see the parking lot though the glass door. It was still light enough outside to make it hard for him to see me watching from inside. The pickpocket looked around before cracking the billfold and pocketing the cabbage. He dropped the wallet into the planter by the door and turned to come back inside. I stepped into an alcove before the door opened. He crossed the room and disappeared into the club, probably heading for the Casino, wherever that was.

I opened the breezeway door and approached the desk clerk. His smile was as pleasant as his holiday tie, but held no promise.

"Where can I find some action?" I asked.

"Whatever do you mean, sir?"

When he shifted his weight on his feet, taking a barely noticeable step to his right, I would've given even odds that he'd stepped on an alert button. The look on the clerk's face might have passed for helpful.

"Perhaps if you are more precise, I could assist you."

I was about to use some two-dollar words to impress the clerk, when a narrow door near the stairwell opened, and a thin man approached. His face was a set of sharp chiseled angles below coal black hair and eyebrows bushy enough to make somebody a nice toupee.

"I'm Leon Consuelo, the manager. May I be of assistance?"

He, too, was apparently not obligated to wear the holiday apparel. He directed me toward the door from which he came.

"If you would step this way, we can talk in private."

I followed him a few feet into the rear of the lobby.

"When I checked in, Frank Torres told me there was gambling. I thought I might try my luck."

"Mr. Torres asked me to inquire as to your intentions before giving you free access to our diversions."

"Tell him that he's worried for nothing. I'm retired. I don't stick my neck out unless I'm paid to do it. There's no percentage in it otherwise. I just want to try a little gambling, to see what I've been missing."

"Just make sure that's all you're here for."

He turned to stand so that we both faced the rear wall. His voice was barely audible.

"Our Casino is on the upper floor of the nightclub. Walk through it on the ocean side, and up the stairs at the far end. Knock on the red door. The password is 'Diamond Jim sent me'."

"Okay, Brother, now I have one for you," I said. "I saw a grifter, about twenty-years-old, pick the pocket of one of your guests. You'll find the empty wallet in the planter outside by the front door. The last I saw, the grifter went into the club."

I gave detailed descriptions of the pickpocket and the victim to Consuelo, who smirked.

"Thanks for the tip. We don't need some punk giving customers reason to worry. We'll take care of this. Enjoy your night at the tables."

He turned toward the club and gestured.

From an alcove near the concierge, two trouble boys emerged, and walked toward us. I walked toward the club, passing them on the way, happy that I didn't trigger any of their alarms.

Chapter Eight

The evergreen festooned stairwell at the rear of the club led up and back to a red-stained wood door. Like something from a medieval fortress, every four inches thick bolts attached a wrought iron grate to the door. Christmas wreaths bracketed a grilled panel set in the door, about head height. I tapped on the panel.

It slid open.

"Yeah?"

I leaned toward the grille and whispered, "Diamond Jim sent me."

The panel snapped shut and after the raspy sound of a heavy bolt being drawn, the thick wooden door opened revealing an unadorned vestibule with another door on the opposite wall.

"Welcome."

The doorman waved me inside and then closed and bolted the door.

"Beer's free if you're gambling. Liquor prices are on the chalkboard behind the bar."

He opened the second door and waved me in. The door swung shut behind me.

It was warm. The lights were dim, but strong enough to illuminate the room. The red velvet walls contrasted with the stamped tin ceiling that reflected the light of six small chandeliers. No "Tin Roof Blues" or traditional Christmas music here. In a rear corner, a Victrola pushed jazz from its megaphone. A kid wearing the requisite red-and-green bow-tie and a pair of white gloves stood by, ready to change the platters, and turn the crank that wound the spring that spun the records that drove the tempo of the gambling in the Roadhouse that Frank built.

Tendrils of Cuban cigar and other good tobacco mixed in air laced with laughter and the tinkling of glasses. Cocktail waitresses in short-skirted elf costumes brought drinks to the men and women at play. Three long craps tables ran down the center of the room, pointing to a bar along the back wall. On the right were three Blackjack tables and two Roulette wheels with a Wheel of Fortune next to the bar. The left wall held rows of slots, Pacinko, and pinball machines. At the far end of the bar, a Christmas tree was covered in frosted white ornaments and sparkling lights. There was no bank window; the gamblers used real money. Police raids left no time for cashing in chips.

The evening was just getting started, and while the room wasn't crowded, the party was already in full swing. Shouts accompanied each throw of the dice, and each spin of the game wheels.

The Depression had thinned the ranks of gamblers. Most of the people with money left to burn were in the social register — the kind who spend their lives conjugating the verb "to idle," the type of people who hire the American Detective Agency to sort out their affairs. I recognized many of the faces. Newspaper society pages were packed with their pictures, and it pays to know your clients.

A clutch of Hunters played Blackjack at the front table, while a band of Kuhns and McGregors tried their luck at Roulette. A troupe of Millers and Mhoons were at the first craps table, the Murphy clan laid siege at the middle table, while a few Dunns and Moffitts played at the one in back. A gaggle of Chandlers played at the middle Blackjack table, and a brace of Rothschilds and Schillings cast their lots at the rear Roulette wheel. A couple of Sperrys circulated while a half-score of Ghirardellis chatted at the bar. None of the five Spreckels families listed in the Social Register were in attendance. I wondered when the blackmailer would drive away enough high-rollers for Frank Torres to take notice.

Unless Torres was in on it, and getting enough to make up for the missing players.

I must have looked idle, or wandered too near the first craps table, because Jack Mhoon waved me over.

"Hi, friend, c'mon over and help us with this bottle. There's not a lot, but there's one more all around."

Once noticed, you'll make a bigger scene declining than accepting, especially when the one offering is gin-tight.

"Sure, got a spare glass?"

I drifted to the table's rail as he took one from a passing elf-waitress' tray. He poured me a slug, and topped a few glasses near him.

"*Slange!*"

He raised his glass; we all did, too.

One of the Miller *débutantes* winked and flirted with two Schilling boys who lolled in the aisle. Though everyone was dressed to the nines, none of the guests was wearing the traditional red and green holiday colors. Apparently, only the help did that. My tux blended in just fine with the social set.

"New shooter," said the croupier as he pushed the dice to a woman standing next to me at the end of the table.

Judging by looks, she was the *débutantes'* mother or aunt. She was tall, five-foot nine, with brown hair and eyes done *à la* Marlene. About thirty-five and thin, but curvy enough to suggest a fertility goddess sculpture. Her cowl-necked dress draped loose and tight in all the appropriate places.

"I'm right tonight," she sang, and then put five dollars on the table. "And my fin is in."

"But it's faded!" snapped a man from across the table.

She paused, without smiling, to regard him.

"I'm backing the house," he said as he put a matching bill on the table.

"Why, James Crabbe, look at you betting on craps!"

She turned to me, her smile back in place.

"Blow me some luck, Mister."

With the dice clamped between her index finger and thumb, she proffered them under my nose. I blew a soft whistle onto her hand. Her well-defined brow arched before she refocused on the game.

"All right, babies, a little seven for mama."

She shook them side-armed, her glittering bracelets jangling, and then let them bounce down the table. From behind, her low-cut gown revealed her long, slim back as she waited, bent over the table, for the dice to come to a stop.

"Seven," cried the croupier, placing another five dollar bill next to her bet and collecting the losing wagers all around.

"Yes!"

She flashed me a smile.

"We doubled my fin."

She looked across the table.

"Jimbo, are you going to keep betting against me?"

"Most assuredly."

"In that case, here's more to keep the others warm."

She tossed a sawbuck onto her wager.

"The shooter bets twenty," the croupier said.

The crowd *oohed* and *ahhed*.

She faced me.

"You're my charm. Let's show Jimbo what getting lucky looks like."

Five throws all went her way, and revealed Jimbo a sore loser. She poured herself into it, adding to her bet every throw, triumph flitting across her face. More people crowded in to watch her betting bout with Jimbo.

Such luck couldn't last.

"Better go easy," I cautioned.

"I don't like it easy," she whispered near my ear. "I like it hard and fast."

She had six to make.

"Spot me."

After I whistled at her hand, she readied her throw.

"Rollin' bones, take me home."

Her luck held, and she made her point. Flushed and half-hysterical, she kissed my cheek. I guessed my luck was rolling, too.

Her next throw was nine, but she couldn't make that point. She lost the dice and the pile of dough that had been rising on the table.

"Lady Luck took a powder. Oh, well!"

She nudged me with her shoulder.

"C'mon, let's dangle."

She put her arm through mine and took a small step away from the table, about a grand lighter in her purse. Her pearl stud earrings — each topped by a carat diamond — perfectly matched the long strand of pearls wrapped once around her neck, its diamond clasp against her throat in front, with the remaining rope of pearls knotted between her shoulders and straying down her bared back. The pearls swayed along with the delicate movement of the gown's bias-cut over her slender hips.

Her movements were tracked by a young man at the table, his eyes following her hips, back, breasts. Maybe he was watching that pearl necklace, too. The kid was little more than a teenager, with sandy brown hair and brown eyes that matched his double-breasted brown suit. His fair skin was as cream-colored as his shirt, tie, and the handkerchief folded perfectly in his suit coat pocket. Perfectly dressed college students like him were called "Joe Brooks."

It's not that my gambling partner didn't have a chassis worth looking over: it's that the Joe Brooks seemed too young to be appraising her. He didn't seem to notice me as we passed, though the woman held my arm almost possessively.

"Where are we going?" I asked.

"Where do you want to take me?"

I led us toward the bar in the back.

"I can think of three different answers, but tell me your name before I choose one."

"I'm Joan Miller, and you are?"

"Then you're also Mrs. Paul Miller."

"Paul died last year in Africa, on a safari."

"My condolences."

"How do you know who I am, but not know Paul is dead?"

I gave her my card.

"I was a detective, but I retired. I've been in Mexico for the last year."

She read it before releasing my arm to put the card in her purse, giving me one of her cards in return, which I pocketed.

Her eyes searched my face.

"It's good for a young widow to count among her friends a man who can be discrete."

I didn't know what her game was, flirting with me. Fillies like her don't stay with aging, short, fat detectives. Not after everybody sobers up.

Never mind: for the moment, I was in luck. Squiring the Miller widow around would provide me cover while I searched for savvy-fare on the blackmailer that preyed on her kind.

We reached the bar, edged with evergreen garlands. She perched on a barstool while I leaned sideways on the bar rail, giving me a view of the room. A few stools down, the pickpocket I'd seen in the lobby left his perch, a beer in hand. I followed him with my eyes.

The Miller dame noticed my gaze and turned back to me.

"A friend of yours?"

"Not if I can help it."

The pickpocket took a chair at the rear Blackjack table. He dropped his bankroll and took a drink of beer.

I turned back to my new friend.

"What'll you have?"

"I can't stand rum, so the Mary Pickford and Planter's Punch cocktails are out. I'm tired of the Orange Blossom I was drinking at the table. That leaves either Scotch, Canadian Rye, or gin cut with whatever mixers are at hand."

"You're a regular," I ventured.

"Almost a fixture," she said. "I'll have their Tom Collins."

I shook two cigarettes from my pack. She held my hand and then put her lips around one of the smokes.

I thumb-struck a wooden match, lighting hers before mine. Her cheeks hollowed as she sucked some smoke and then blew out the match. Her eyes held mine for a moment before I tossed the spent matchstick into an ashtray on the bar. We both inhaled deeply. The smoke curled into my lungs, scratching an itch I barely noticed was there.

She waved, as if to dismiss something.

"The City was dreary, so we came here to shake a leg."

Why was she being so friendly? I decided it must be the liquor talking. After smoothing my coat sleeve, she held my hand. Maybe she was looking for an emotional anchor, and I looked old and slow enough to be one.

"Most of us are here for four days," she said, giving me a sultry look, "but I might stay longer."

She half-smiled, looking down as she fiddled with one of my coat buttons.

"How long are you staying?"

"I don't know yet," I said.

One of the bartenders sidled over to take our order. Apparently, only the cocktail waitresses had to dress as if they worked the North Pole. The bartender wore the same basic uniform as all the male help at the Roadhouse: black shoes, pants, and vest; crisp white shirt; red-and-green plaid bow-tie with silver and gold threads. I added a Rye and soda to her Tom Collins.

"Prohibition has Kentucky locked down tight. What I'd do for a real bourbon and branch water..."

Her eyes held mine as she spoke again.

"Or a shot of tequila."

Before I could answer, movement at the front caught my eye. Two trouble boys from downstairs — the ones whom the floor manager had tasked to take care of the pickpocket — entered and scanned the room. Both still sported their fedoras. I picked the closest one, and waited for his eyes to lock onto mine.

When they did, I nodded. He raised and lowered his eyebrows. I turned my head to look at the pickpocket.

A minute later, the two trouble boys stood behind the pickpocket on either side of his chair. I nodded again. One of them reached over the kid's left shoulder and took his cash.

The kid turned, following the money. His "Hey!" was loud enough to crest the crowd noise. Apparently, whatever the second one whispered into the kid's ear convinced him to behave. The three of them walked to the back wall, where one of the curtains concealed a door.

I turned to Mrs. Miller, just as our drinks arrived. I paid the bartender.

"What did you just do?" she asked.

"I bought us a drink. If you're nice to me, I'll do it again."

"Not the drinks. What did you do to that young man playing Blackjack?"

"I don't know what you mean."

"You just gave an order to a pair of brunos who hauled him away. Are you part of the mob that runs this joint?"

"No, I'm retired, and from the right side of the law, too."

Wrapped in silence, her eyes fixed on mine, I surmised that she wouldn't let it go without an explanation.

"I saw the kid lift a guest's wallet. I informed the manager, who sent some gents out to find him. What you saw was me confirming that they had the right guy."

"I hope you don't turn *me* in for anything."

She flipped her naturally wavy hair back, exposing the one-carat diamond set above the pearl in her earring, and setting the drapery of her silk gown swaying. Along with the pearl necklace down the center of her bare back.

Back to the flirting *divertissement.*
I stepped closer and lowered my voice.
"Spill it," I said. "What's your game?"

Chapter Nine

*N*o game," she said with a pout.

"Don't try to con a pro, Sweetheart."

"You're different," she said. "I like different."

Her eyes shone.

"It's as if you've already had your fun."

Her perfume was lavender, the imported kind.

"Okay, I'll play," I said. "Give me the 'According to Hoyle's'."

"If I were your stool pigeon..."

"What makes you think I need a stoolie?"

"Doesn't every lawman?" she said, blinking her smoky-shadowed, *à la* Dietrich eyes.

"Even if I needed one, why would I want you?"

"Because I've got the goods on everyone in here."

"Even the pickpocket?"

"This was his first night in here, but I could find out his name if you want."

I took a long drink, and then a long drag, holding the smoke in my lungs as I stared at her. I let the smoke out slow. She didn't move.

"What would you get out of it?"

"You couldn't turn me in."

"For what?"

"For anything."

I gave her my most endearingly crooked smile.

"Is that your best offer?"

She shrugged her shoulders, mostly bare except for the thin straps of her gown.

"I could be your moll."

"What will I tell my regular girl?"

"Now who's kidding whom?" she asked, laughing pleasantly before she picked up her drink and sipped it.

"Okay, you're in. You start tonight as my pigeon. You can work your way up the pecking order."

"Where do I begin?" she asked, adjusting herself on the barstool so she was closer to me even as she surveyed the room's occupants.

"We don't want to fall asleep just yet. Start with something salacious."

"Something juicy, eh? Okay, see the man with the mustachio standing at the Wheel of Fortune? The one wearing the white bow-tie with his tux. That's Dirk Ferguson. His wife, Marian, has the blonde pin-curls, and is at the rear Roulette table, standing with her back to us, wearing the Midnight blue dress with matching fringe. The one who looks like she's still a flapper."

She had the stilts for it. I nodded.

"In about ten minutes Marian will leave, claiming to be tired. Instead, she'll spend a few hours between the sheets in their chauffeur's room."

"What's Mr. Ferguson say to that?"

"He won't notice. He'll be too busy in Trudy Palmer's room. She's the curling-iron brunette wearing a sleek brown halter-dress at the end of the bar, near Ferguson."

"The one with the emeralds?"

"That's her."

"Is there a Mr. Palmer?"

"Yes, but he's... flamboyant."

I looked at her without blinking. She arched her eyebrows and tilted her head.

"He's an... Ethel."

"I'm not following you, Sister."

She held her hand up, then let her braceleted-wrist go limp.

I rolled my eyes.

She nodded.

"Yes, and he was careless. Trudy was such a poor, poor little bunny after she and a few weekend house-guests discovered him... you know..."

"*In flagrante delicto?*"

"It hit her like a Chicago typewriter," said the Miller widow, sipping her drink. "Finding out that her husband was an inveterate skirt-chaser would have been better than discovering that he's a three-letter-man."

I motioned the bartender for another Rye and soda while Mrs. Miller continued.

"After that, Chas spent more time away from home — not at the club — leaving poor little Trudy bunny alone with her self-doubts. She's using Dirk to prove to herself that it wasn't any lack of feminine charm on her part that made Chas… that way."

"Did Mr. Palmer come down this trip?"

"No, Chas is probably with his 'friend' in Sausalito, a ferry ride north…"

"…of The City," I said with her.

I shook two more Fatimas up in the pack. She shook her head. I lit one for myself.

"How do you know all of this?"

"I'm a good listener. Besides, a widow needs a hobby, doesn't she?"

"I'm sure the butler or gardener could lend a hand."

"And have *them* gossip about *me?* Not on your life."

She slid her fingers under my shirtsleeve and lightly rubbed the inside of my wrist.

"But with a professional peeper, I could start a new hobby."

"Now who's kidding whom?" I asked, looking at her ticklers under my cuff.

She withdrew her hand.

"Why? You don't like girls, or is it just me?"

"I like women just fine, but I'm skeptical that you want the likes of me."

She smiled and patted my stomach.

"You're a Baby-Grand, that's for sure, but what makes you think I don't prefer a handful?"

I blew smoke away from her face.

"The socials have become tedious: too many of the same faces and the same routines. We need some new blood, some excitement."

The bartender slid my next drink over.

The Miller widow leaned in close and lowered her voice.

"After Paul passed, my mourning period was rough."

I waited.

"Discovering that I prefer… unsafe partners was liberating."

"Unsafe?"

"I quit looking for pretty boys and started seeking the more dicey kind."

"Do you like to feel unsafe?"

"Sometimes."

The right side of her lips curled into a half-smile.

"Don't worry. It's all 'According to Hoyle's', as you say, so nobody really gets hurt."

She gave me a sultry look from the top of her eyes.

"You're not like the others," she purred. "You're interesting. And I can tell you're dangerous."

She seemed to want me to say something, but it wasn't for me to explain her mind.

"See? Men usually jump in, pushing for the prize, but not you. You're not selling anything."

She paused to give me a sidelong glance.

"But you *are* working an angle."

"And what's that?" I asked.

"I don't know yet."

"When you figure it out, let me know."

"I will," she said, looking at me over her drink.

Cayte, the maid from my room, in a long sapphire-blue dress, entered the bar through the curtained door. She waved to a bartender, who brought her a martini, *sans* olive. She sat on a stool at the end of the bar near the Casino's Christmas tree. I kept an eye on her while I had another drink, and chatted with my pigeon.

"Your first story was jake," I said. "Tell me another."

"Okay. It's not as juicy," said Mrs. Miller, "but it's a scandal nonetheless."

Cayte sipped her drink, watching the door from her stool perch. The Miller widow watched her social set at the various tables. The brown-haired, teenaged Forty-Niner watched Mrs. Miller. I watched, too.

Chapter Ten

*M*rs. Miller started in on another story about love and betrayal, but I was more interested in the events taking place around us. A young woman in a simple but rather elegant white dress joined Cayte at the bar, leaning in close as she waited for her drink. The woman didn't look like a socialite, and she didn't appear to be with any of them either: no expensive jewelry. Cayte smiled at something the woman said, but I didn't catch it with the Widow's story sounding in my other ear.

Just as I changed position, I thought I caught a glimpse of the young woman touching Cayte's arm, but she might have just bumped her as she turned away with her own drink: it looked like a Sidecar with a twist of lemon zest on the rim of the martini glass.

Just then, Contina, in his long-tailed concert coat and ruffled shirt that he wore at the piano, emerged from the curtained doorway behind the bar. As he joined Cayte for drinks, the bartender had Contina's martini ready. Cayte touched the piano player's face, and he turned to her. Her arms went around his neck and, as they kissed, he held her waist. I looked up but didn't see any mistletoe. Round One of their wrestling match over, they resumed talking and drinking. Though the Joe Brooks Forty-Niner divided his gaze between them and the Miller widow, Cayte and Contina paid him no attention. Neither did Mrs. Miller.

The front door opened and two couples entered. I recognized the man leading the group as the pickpocket's victim. They were headed our way. Our end of the bar was the least crowded.

I interrupted the Miller widow.

"Let's eavesdrop on the couples that are about to join us. You might get a kick out of it."

"See? I told you, you were one of the dicey ones."

Her smile was wry, but still lovely.

They drew near.

"It's our lucky night. I can feel it," said the woman on the arm of the victim.

"It must be. When the manager returned my wallet, it had an extra fifty dollars in it."

His smile looked bigger than his face.

"The drinks are on me!"

"Let's scoot, Sweet-cheeks," I said, taking Mrs. Miller's hand. "And let them have a chance at the spigot."

"Okay, Darling," she said.

We took our drinks farther down the bar, then turned into the room. The brown-haired teen Forty-Niner stood and walked toward the restrooms.

"Were those the folks who you saw get clipped?" she asked.

"The same."

"Maybe you *are* one of the good guys."

"Don't go placing your bets, Sweetheart."

Contina and Cayte placed their empty glasses on the bar, stood, and, holding hands, left through the curtained door in the back.

"What's through the door in back?" I asked.

"What makes you think I know?"

"You're the fixture here. Want to show me where it goes?"

"We can explore it together. Do you think we'll get caught?"

"Maybe."

"How exciting."

She turned and walked to the back, placing her empty glass on the bar as she passed. I followed the sway of her hips that were keeping time with the Victrola, losing my highball glass onto a table along the way.

Upon reaching the exit, she pulled the curtain aside to reveal a door. I tried the knob; it wasn't locked, and opened onto a corridor. I waved her past me, scanning the bar. Nobody I could see cared if we used the service port. Out of habit, I tried the door handle again as soon as it closed behind us. It was locked. With no key, we would need another route back in.

The unadorned corridor was illuminated every ten feet by bare bulbs in the ceiling. Dark scuff marks marred the off-white paint, and a few deep gouges exposed the lath below the plaster wall.

"They must save the gingerbread for the public," she said.

"Yeah, it's like that all over."

I stepped in front of her.

"Want to see where this goes? I'm game."

"Yeah, but are you in season?" she said while patting my ass.

I turned to give her a blank stare.

She returned it in deadpan.

"You need to loosen up."

"Maybe I need another drink."

"Whatever you need isn't in this corridor."

She stepped out.

"Let's go."

I quick-stepped and got in front of her.

"You'd better let me go first: there may be surprises."

"Such as?"

"It's not the Mark Hopkins on Nob Hill; it's a mob joint."

That finally gave her pause.

"Maybe you should go first," she said.

I tried the first door on the left. A small closet held cleaning supplies and a mop bucket.

"Ooh, scary," she said.

I closed the door. The next door on the left was a large storage room with spare dining tables and chairs, and stacks of dish boxes against the wall. Next was a stairwell. Faint sounds of dishes banging and raised voices reached our ears.

"Now I'm really getting frightened," she said from behind my shoulder. "I may need to cling to you in my panic."

Across from the stairwell was a door in the right side wall. It opened to a balcony. We stepped outside.

"It's chilly."

She wrapped herself in her arms.

"We won't be long."

I took off my coat and wrapped it around her shoulders.

Her nose sought the warmth of my chest. Over her shoulder I saw two people huddled on the bluff below. Except for the woman's long gown glittering blue in the moonlight, I wouldn't have guessed who they were. Mrs. Miller turned to follow my gaze. The couple merged into one shape, heads close together.

"They look happy," she said.

Contina hadn't proffered his coat to Cayte.

"She'll get cold soon," I said.

The lovers broke their clinch, and hurried to the breezeway that connected the club to the hotel.

"They'll be warm soon enough," she said.

Before the entendre doubled-down, I steered her back through the door and into the corridor. Once inside, she gave me my coat. I put it on and continued to the door at the end. A stairway led down to the breezeway lobby.

"That certainly was exciting. And so very dangerous. I'm so glad you were here to protect me."

"Maybe we can scare up some trouble tomorrow."

"Tomorrow? The night's still young."

Marian Ferguson exited the club and crossed the breezeway to the hotel building's door.

I pulled the Miller widow deeper into the shadow of a large potted ficus, painted glass-bird Christmas ornaments with white tail feathers clipped to its branches. If the Miller widow was right, Blonde-Pin-Curls in the Midnight-Blue-with-fringe was on her way to her chauffeur's room.

"I'm tired from traveling all day," I said. "I think I'll turn in early."

"You're telling me the Bank's closed already?"

She was still flirting with me.

"Cash or check?" she said, lifting her face slightly.

I wasn't giving her a kiss then, or a promise of one later. She raised her eyes toward the ceiling.

"There's mistletoe," she said.

I said nothing, and I didn't look up.

She pouted, but in an attractive way.

"I'll see you at breakfast?"

"Goodnight, Mrs. Miller."

She extended her hand.

"Please, call me Joan."

After a brief touch, she disappeared into the club.

I entered the hotel. Mrs. Pin-Curls wasn't in the first floor corridor. I trotted up the stairs. The fringe on the hem of her dress swished into the doorway of a room half-way down the row. I walked briskly and then pressed my ear for a listen. Even through a wooden door, sweet nothings still have a distinctive sound. I listened at the doors on each side of her assignation. No sound came from either room.

I walked toward the lobby to retrieve my overcoat and hat, wondering if the card game was in Edward "Kid" Ory's room, or if I'd find the drummer hosting the action tonight.

Chapter Eleven

I woke in a fit of coughing, not from smoke or Nevada gas fogging my room, but from a heavy smoker's need to expel the lung gunk that comes with the habit. Of late, my morning coughs were taking longer to clear, and now produced some blood. I washed it down the drain and took a quick bath.

Toweling off, I saw that room service had delivered a tray of coffee and rolls, setting it on the table next to the Poinsettia. My room at the Marine View Hotel was on the end nearest the club, giving me a side window that the interior rooms lacked. From my vantage point, I drank java and watched the morning's commerce while I avoided The Depression headlines on the newspaper.

Trucks of various sizes pulled off the highway to ply their wares. Meat from Chicago slaughterhouses shipped through the railhead in San José arrived concurrently with farm-fresh produce trucked in from the south. Fish, bread, and canned goods arrived from points north. The laundry truck was from San Bruno, just south of San Francisco: that's a long way to go for clean tablecloths and bedding when there were suitable companies in closer cities.

I was debating whether to visit the dining room for steak and eggs, or just order room service when a murder of crows emerged from the breezeway lobby. The swirl of black suits separated into individual humans who broke into three flocks, each on its way to a line of Packards parked in the lot. One set took two cars and turned north toward Muscle Shoals. Three cars went south toward Año Nuevo. The last three out of the lot went north, but before they crested the ridge, they turned right onto a gravel road that went east over the hill. If that road went through, it would hit the Bay somewhere near Palo Alto.

The trail of clues wasn't getting warmer. I put on a fresh collar along with a light gray suit without the vest, and went to see who was sober or hung-over in the morning. I found my way into the dining room and ordered a pot of java before I had my napkin in my lap. When the waitress returned, I ordered the Roadhouse's version of the Blue Plate breakfast, and then looked around.

Some folks eat and get on the road; others eat and relax. Despite the economy, everyone was suited up for civilization, but you can tell what folks are going to do for the day by the way the women are dressed. Most of the women were in plain-cloth dresses with loose sleeves, ready for a road-trip home from the Roadhouse. A few wore sundresses, perhaps hoping that the sunlight would break through the ever-present northern Californian gloom. Almost all of them had some bit of makeup on, and some curl in their hair. Virtually all of them were glancing out the windows overlooking the ocean between bites of breakfast and sips of coffee. I hoped that they would find what they sought.

Arbuckle and Keaton chatted at their table. Miss Page, in a cream blouse and a tweed skirt, with her hair curled under this morning, and Montgomery, in full suit and tie, entered the dining room. Both seemed to be in a state of agitation.

"What's wrong?"

"Nothing," said Montgomery, pulling out a chair for Miss Page.

"We can't find Bob's wallet," blurted the starlet.

"I asked you not to say anything," said Montgomery, pushing aside the menu as he sat.

"I'll pay your bill," Arbuckle offered.

"I couldn't accept."

"I insist."

The girl smiled at Montgomery.

"Thank you, Mr. Arbuckle," he said.

"I thought we settled it that you'd call me 'Roscoe'."

Now there was a real butter-and-egg man. I turned my attention to the rest of the room, but the San Francisco socialites were apparently not morning people. Without them, I would have to look elsewhere for leads. Though the morning sun over the ocean and beach made a pleasant view, I had a job to do, so I finished my breakfast, signed for it, brushed off any crumbs from my pants legs with my napkin, then left the table.

I went to the parking lot and smoked three Fatimas while watching the random acts of commerce that occurred. Nothing seemed unusual, so I took my Nicotine-fortified self to an unexplored clue from the night before. I entered the breezeway lobby, and with nobody around, I slipped through the door that led upstairs to the hallway that connected to the back of the Casino's gambling salon.

The corridor was empty. I made my way to the last door on the left that opened onto the small cleaning supply closet. I turned on the light and closed the door behind me. I bent and inspected the large mop sink. Subtle scrape marks were visible on the floorboards.

I found the release button on the wall behind the Bon Ami scouring powder that sat on the shelf. I pressed and held the button. The mop sink slid to the right, revealing a dark opening onto a spiral staircase. The light switch was on a post just below the room's floor level. I descended.

I could not see the bottom, but the exposed ropes and pulleys of a pair of dumbwaiters were evident. Based on the positions, the top of these rudimentary elevators must be in the storage room next door to the mop room.

As I approached the bottom, I could hear the sounds of surf. In the dim light coming from the west, I could make out stacked boxes of booze against the wall. Bacardi white rum — probably from Cuba via Mexico — Canadian Whiskey, Martini's Noilly Prat vermouth, Grenadine, Gordon's Gin, cases of quinine-filled tonic water. All that was missing were the lemon zest, the maraschino cherries, and the chilled, sugar-rimmed crystal glasses.

What light there was in the storeroom came from what must have been a waterway to the ocean. The man-made channel went west then turned south, undoubtedly making a few turns before exiting the grotto, so as to make a sheltered harbor.

The sounds of an engine came from the water.

"Grab the line and get ready to pull us in."

The motor sputtered and went out. Three voices conversed on the status of warping the boat into the dock below my feet. I retreated a few spirals up the staircase where the shadows were deeper.

"Murphy said to unload these cases here, and not to mention to Patroni, why we didn't use his dock. *Capisce?*"

"Yeah, we got it."

"Mum's the word."

Not wanting to step on a loose or creaking board, I stood still on my perch until they had finished. Fortunately, they went back from whence they came, never venturing toward the staircase. Once they were outside, the engine coughed to life and faded into the distance.

I returned aloft to the mop room, where I doused the light and triggered the mechanism to return the mop sink to where it covered the hatch to the spiral staircase.

I listened at the door. Hearing nothing, I opened it and stepped into the corridor. Just as I closed it, the door to the gambling hall opened, and a young man backed into the corridor, listening to someone in the bar.

"Go to the basement and check to see if those cases of Scotch were delivered."

I had already made my way into the storage room next to the mop room and closed the door when the young man acknowledged his task. I hid behind one of the large tables that stood on its side and waited.

The door opened. The young man accessed a tall and wide Armoire, and then flipped up the bottom. He left the way he came. Sounds from next door could be heard.

I waited a few minutes for him to get down the staircase before leaving my hiding place. I went to the Armoire and looked down. It was too dim to see anything, so I opened the door to the corridor and turned left, making my way back to the hotel's breezeway.

I hurried, hoping to avoid being spotted.

Chapter Twelve

I made my way back to my room, where the maid, Cayte, along with another maid, were working. More precisely, Cayte was busy cleaning while the other girl was sitting on the end of the bed talking to her. As soon as I entered, the second girl jumped up — almost losing the holly sprig behind her name-tag — and slipped from the room. After I'd calmed Cayte's startled state at my return, she started to talk.

"That's Anna, the girl who lets me stay with her," she said, tucking her hair behind her ear. "The one Johnny... John... Mr. Contina introduced me to."

I asked her a question to give her focus.

"How do you like your job?"

"It's okay, I guess. I'd like something better, but I need to hide from my husband..."

"He doesn't already know where you are?"

She shook her head, glancing toward the windows.

"His temper... he'll kill me if he finds me."

"What about Contina? Why doesn't he take you away from all this?"

"John? Why would you ask about John?"

"The two of you appear to be an item."

"I don't know what you mean. We're just friendly."

"Okay, but as a friend, he could see about giving you an out for your situation."

"I couldn't ask him; he's already done so much for me, getting me this job, finding me a friend with a spare room to stay in, giving me some money when I arrived until I got my first paycheck. I just couldn't ask him for anything more."

"Suit yourself, Sister, but if he's jake with you, he needs to give you an out, and not just enjoy your sugar."

"I don't need another husband."

"First one's that bad?"

Her chin quivered. I needed to change the subject.

"But you like your job?"

"It's okay, but I wouldn't want to do it for the rest of my life. It's pretty much routine."

"Yeah, pretty much every day would be like the previous, depending on which rooms are occupied. Besides the routine, are there any rooms that are irregular, that give you something different each day?"

"Well, there's a suite of rooms closer to where the girls work in the brothel... One room near there is never really used, but I still have to clean it."

"What do you mean, exactly?"

"The bed's never slept in, but the ashtrays are usually full, and they always want fresh towels. Next door, the room itself is always clean, except sometimes the bed looks like an army slept in it."

"That's a fun one. What about the bathroom in that room?"

"Always in perfect order. That's one of the strange things about it."

"Any other interesting rooms?"

"There's one where it looks like men just play poker and drink all night. The table's always covered with glasses and empty bottles, the ashtrays are overflowing, and the floor's a mess."

"What about the bed in that room?"

"Never touched. But the bathroom's always filthy. I'm supposed to leave extra towels and soap in that one."

"Any others?"

"Not that I can think of right now, but I'm just one of the maids. I could ask the others if you want."

"No, that's fine. So, who was that helping you clean my room when I came in?"

"Oh, Anna wasn't helping me," said Cayte, blushing. "She's my roommate, like I told you. We were just talking about something."

"You're the only maid cleaning my room?"

"That's just the rotation. One of the other maids will do your room when we switch floors," she said before she stopped dusting the table and straightened up. "I could stay as your maid if you request me."

"I may just do that."

"That would be awfully nice of you. The supervisor notices when girls get asked for. That would help me keep my job, make a little more money, and get back on my feet without having to ask anyone for favors or help."

Her smile almost warmed my stone heart.

"Shouldn't you be getting to your luncheon?" she asked.

"I haven't worked off breakfast yet."

She smiled, pulling the sheets off the bed.

"But if you wait too long, you'll get the overcooked rump end."

I stood. I watched her re-make the bed, wondering if she was still playing me. I hoped she wasn't. She seemed like a sweet kid, and I didn't want her to be a grifter.

Chapter Thirteen

I nside the dining hall, the hostess showed me to a table. I gave the waiter my order for the pot roast special of the day and sat back to enjoy the coffee. I'd barely lifted the chilled cover over the butter and spread the creamy white over the fresh-baked bread when Frank Torres appeared at my side. I took a big bite out of the crusty bread with the fresh butter before he could say anything.

"You visited my tables."

I nodded.

"Win anything?"

"I didn't play. Just served as somebody's lucky charm. Till her luck ran out."

"It happens," said Torres.

"You've got a Dip."

"Not anymore."

"You turn him over?"

"No need to involve anyone else. The ocean currents are strong along here."

He gave me his horse-faced smile. I pulled apart another piece of the bread, flakes from its double-crust scattering around the basket, and then buttered the bread. It was better than the flour or corn *tortillas* I'd gotten used to. And the butter was so fresh, it hadn't had a chance to turn yellow. I looked for my waiter, my mouth watering for that pot roast special. Torres wasn't finished with me yet.

"What do you think of my club?"

"Very festive. Especially the bow-ties. And all the elves have great gams."

He continued with the straight look.

"Your club looks legit," I said.

"Why do you sound surprised?"

"I'm surprised that you're resisting the trend to mix big cons with your gambling."

Torres made a face and a dismissive gesture.

"Other houses might try that stuff, but a big con takes time to set up and resources to run."

"Not enough time," I said, seeing my waiter approach, "or not enough resources?"

"Not enough patience for that sort of affair," said Torres. "I've got a Roadhouse to run, profits to make on the hooch, and I don't tolerate people poaching game in my preserve."

He smiled again.

"So, are you up on me, or has the house been keeping some of your spare change?"

"I'm down a little. Mostly drinks. But I seem to be making up for it from your kitchen."

"Here's your meal," he said as my waiter arrived.

A covered hot plate was placed in front of me, and a chilled salad bowl next to that. The waiter picked up the bread-basket and the china butter server, set them on the tray he held up in the air on his left hand, and placed a fresh basket of bread — covered with one of the thick napkins — and another chilled butter dish on the table. After he inquired whether I wanted my drink refreshed, he bowed his head slightly and departed. I took the lid off the entrée, closing my eyes as the steam from the pot roast and the dark gravy over the mashed potatoes wafted toward my face. Torres laughed softly.

"Enjoy yourself," he said as he left.

I did. The food here was better than the hooch. As I ate, I watched the floor show. A group of designers was showing its wares on an impromptu fashion runway to one side of the dining hall. Several of the women I'd seen in the Casino were now watching lithe young models strut up and down the walkway.

The skirts were longer at the back than the front. Below the knee, pleats and godets fell from panels, providing fullness at the hemline that grazed the bottom of the calf. Strawberry-red, sunflower-yellow, and new-money-green were mixed among multitudinous shades of blue. Of course, the ubiquitous white, cream, silver, and gold were also adequately represented. The draped fabric looked like rayon or nylon, one of the new fabrics invented by man.

Whatever it was, it looked good on the models, especially when they moved.

Laced, suede pumps appeared beside black-and-white cut-out oxfords on the make-shift runway. The decorated T-strap, two-button *Fasenettas*, and the white-suede T-strap with the ankle-strap were among my favorites. I liked to see a little foot with a dame's gams.

Joan Miller was among the women at the fashion show. I ate my pot roast, mashed potatoes with lots of gravy, and braised carrots, and let the situation evolve. I heard familiar voices entering the dining area.

"But what about your new film?"

I turned to see Buster Keaton and Roscoe Arbuckle being shown to a nearby table.

"*Up a Tree?* has been out for almost a month," replied Arbuckle.

"No, I mean what you have planned for next year. What's on the slate?"

"It's going to be a busy year. I'm ambitious, and hope that making twenty films for E. W. Hammons at Educational Pictures will pave the way for my comeback."

Their waiters filled the glasses on the table with ice-studded water. After Arbuckle ordered a French-75, and Keaton, a Southside, they resumed their conversation. Again, Arbuckle took one of the rosebuds from the centerpiece and slipped it into his buttonhole. I thought about doing the same but reminded myself I was wearing my casual suit. I sipped my second Sidecar, and ostensibly admired the models while unobtrusively listening to the men talk. Eavesdropping was more fun than watching the fashion show, now in its third parade of dresses and shoes.

"I've got Ernie Pagano writing about half of them," said Arbuckle. "The first few are standard fare, but *Crashing Hollywood* is one to bet on. Betty Grable's a girl in the chorus line, but she has great potential. I'm helping her get started."

"Mary Brooks made a big splash last year in *Pandora's Box*. I got the director, Georg Pabst, to recommend a light comedy between her dramatic roles. She will star in *Windy Riley Goes Hollywood*.

"I'm going to slip myself into *The Back Page*, to test the waters for my return to acting. I won't take a credit, but if I can show the studios that my face on screen won't scare away the audience, then I've made progress."

After their drinks arrived, the stars ordered the luncheon special. Glancing at the amateur fashion models, Keaton pointed out one or two of the dresses, while Arbuckle nodded. Neither looked out at the ocean view from the dining room windows, though the sun was now glinting off the water as it rolled onto the white sand beach. Keaton ate his bread without butter as the two continued talking business.

"I'm directing one of my own stories, *That's My Line*. It should be ready mid-summer. I'm hoping that RKO will make it a series about traveling salesmen. And I've cast George Chandler in two films. Do you know him?"

"No, I don't think so," replied Keaton.

"When I first read his name, I had an intuition... something about his name seemed familiar. No matter, he's been in a string of one- and two-reelers: he'll be fine."

"The rest are too far into the future to wager on them, but you know how it is, we'll just wing it."

The fashion show was now over and the models, departing, passing by my table on the way out. As I watched the congregants dissipate, the Miller widow locked her gaze onto me. I had nothing else to do, so I accepted the invitation to look.

She took that as an offer, and came my way. I motioned to one of the waiters standing against the wall, who arrived before the lady.

"Yes, sir?"

"I'd like a pitcher of Martinis," I said.

"Why not make that a pitcher of Mint Juleps?" the Miller widow suggested. "You know, like in *The Great Gatsby*."

"Whatever makes the lady happy," I said.

"Yes, sir. Right away."

I stood and pulled a chair for her that would give her a view of the ocean, the sun-sparkling waves, and the cliff. She smiled and sat.

"So, what did Mrs. Miller think of the fashion show?"

"Please! Call me Joan, or Joanie: I insist!"

"Okay, but only when we're alone. I wouldn't want any gossip to get started."

"Maybe I need some scandal. It's been boring without Paul."

"How did Mr. Miller die?"

"He loved adventure. His cousin Jimbo…"

"James Crabbe?"

"That's him. Jimbo roped Paul into a Kenyan Colony investment. My uncle Silas cautioned against it. He thought the Brits had the colony all sewn up, but Jimbo insisted. Paul and he went to Kenya."

Clearly Mrs. Miller was ready to tell this tale. I motioned her for more of the story just as the pitcher of Mint Juleps and the chilled glasses arrived. She took a long drink before she continued.

"Once there, they were warned off by the local Brits. To avoid making it a trip for biscuits, they went on safari. I blame Jimbo for Paul's death: if he hadn't insisted, Paul wouldn't have gone to Africa. He wouldn't have gone on safari, where he died."

Her eyes were wet.

"Now you've made me cry."

"It helps to tell a sad tale enough times to let the sting out."

She dabbed her eyes with a cambric, lace-edged handkerchief.

"How are you doing, now?" I asked.

"Better than I used to. You're such a good listener. Maybe that helps."

"More help is on the way."

I lifted the pitcher and topped off her glass.

She clinked the lip of her glass to mine, and we drank. The Mint Julep was sweet, but with a tart edge; it was quite refreshing.

"You mentioned a need for some scandal. Isn't there enough of it between your social set and the Casino?"

"Spouses playing musical houses and bed-hopping? That's normal run-of-the-mill philandering. For excitement, Paul was the real deal. He knew how to find it! He would take chances on something more than a Roulette wheel or a deck of cards. He would play angles in business that most people didn't see were there. I know you're probably not going to believe this, but his brain was even more exciting than his good looks. At least to me."

"Why wouldn't I believe it? Mr. Miller sounds like a good egg. I would have liked to have known him."

"You two would have gotten on famously."

The Joe Brooks Forty-Niner from the previous night in the Casino came into the dining room and took a seat a few tables down. Wearing a Yale-blue suit with a lighter blue shirt, red tie with white polka dots, and sporting a bright yellow handkerchief in his suit pocket, he sat where his line of sight was behind Joan, who seemed unaware of his presence.

"Would you like to stroll the grounds with me?" she asked. "Maybe we can find some excitement."

"What about the Joe Brooks sitting behind you? He's got excitement and yearning all over him, and it's not for me."

Joan twisted her upper torso slightly as if to survey the room and then casually turned back.

"That Forty-Niner?"

"I thought it was just me, thinking evil thoughts."

"Don't worry about him. He's just a babe in training. Nice stamina. Less discretion, as you probably gathered since you noticed him. I also have to work on his green-eyes."

"They look blue enough from here."

"I meant the metaphorical green-eyed monster."

"I can't say that I blame him."

"Now who's being gallant?"

I stood.

"You're leaving already?"

"I have a few things to take care of. Perhaps we could have supper together tonight?"

"That would be lovely."

As I leaned over the table to sign the bill for lunch and the hooch, I noticed the Joe Brooks pick up his martini and head toward the Miller widow. Just in case he had anything to do with the blackmail scheme, I took Mrs. Miller's hand and pressed a light kiss on the back of it. She flushed pink, but seemed pleased. I passed the frowning teenager as I walked to the hotel lobby. Now he had something to think about.

I already had something more important to think about: my incessant morning cough. I found the phone booth and gave the hotel operator my name and room number. I asked to be connected to Dr. Edward Marz in San Francisco. After a few minutes, the phone buzzed.

"Yes?"

"I have Dr. Marz on the line. Go ahead, Dr. Marz."

It sounded as if the hotel operator hung up, but how could I know for sure?

"This is Dr. Marz. How can I help you?"

"My morning cough is taking longer to clear. I'm coughing up blood."

"That's not good. Do you smoke?"

"Yes, I do."

"You need to come in and let me examine you. Since you called me direct, I assume that you've been a patient of mine before."

"Yes, you've patched me up a few times when I was working for the American Detective Agency. I'm retired now, but you're the only sawbones I know. When can I come by?"

"How about tomorrow afternoon? Say, just after three?"

"I'll see you then."

I tapped the earpiece cradle a few times. The hotel operator came on the line.

"Please connect me to the Bay Point Oyster Company in San Francisco."

I waited until we were connected before asking for Brian O'Doul. After a short wait, I heard O'Doul's gruff tenor brogue.

"What can I be doing for you?"

"You, Palooka, it's me: your old dancing partner."

"Sure, you are. I didn't know you were up-and-up."

"I'm on a stringer for the Old Man."

"Do tell. What is it that you're after?"

"I need information on safari outfitting companies in the British Colony of Kenya. I'm looking for the one used by Paul Miller and his cousin James Crabbe, a.k.a. Jimbo, for their safari."

"You'll be wanting the whole johnny-cake?"

"Not this time. Just the overview. I'll stop by for it tomorrow around supper time."

Chapter Fourteen

*B*ack in my room a few hours later, after I'd slipped off my jacket and undone my collar, the telephone rang. I set my report aside and answered it.

"It's Joanie. You never told me what time we're having supper."

"How about now?"

"Sure. I can stop by your room and we can get started."

"I thought that we were avoiding scandal."

"You're no fun."

"How about I meet you at the supper club in a half-an-hour?" I suggested.

"I'll see you there."

I hung the phone in the cradle and repacked my paperwork into the hidden bottom of my suitcase, then put on a fresh collar and went to supper. I thought about changing suits, but opted to remind the Miller widow that I wasn't a member of her social set. I put the light gray jacket back on, though I added the matching vest underneath.

It was early, but a fair number of people had turned out. I surveyed the room for Mrs. Miller before presenting myself to the hostess. The slender red-head from the other night was on duty. Her neck was still long, and her well-shaped face was still alluring.

"Good evening, sir. What will be your pleasure this evening?"

"I'd like a table for two, toward the side, if you can swing it."

"Oh, I can swing it for you."

I let that flirt fall on the floor as I followed her to a table near the stage. No keyhole opening in the back of her dress tonight: this time, slinky fabric draped from the shoulder straps to the waist, leaving her entire back bare. The view was even better than the one out the windows. She showed me the seats, and I settled in to the one that would allow me to keep an eye the room.

As I waited for Mrs. Miller to arrive, I listened to the conversations around me. The table behind me spoke the loudest, almost drowning out the traditional holiday tunes Contina was playing on the piano.

"Last month, I read about how four New York banks were going to merge into a mega-bank. The President of the New York Federal Reserve was going to be in charge. But today they called the whole thing off. The headline said 'Bank Closes Doors; State Takes Over Affairs.' Mark my words: there will be a run on that bank."

Another voice took up the refrain.

"The market will react negatively to that, and the price of the bank stock will drop like a stone. It will drag other bank stocks down with it."

When a third voice came in, I coughed and looked over, unfolding my napkin and placing it on my left leg as I did so. The table was full of gray-haired men in tuxes. Two wore eyeglasses. The third fiddled with the table settings, despite the fact that there were two half-empty pitchers of martinis within his reach. Their nails were as trimmed as their hair, and buffed as shiny as their shoes.

"No, bank directors will stay optimistic that the bank will reopen in a short time. They have to keep a stiff upper lip and tough it out, hoping to keep their depositors."

The first voice cut in. It belonged to the most distinguished looking man of the group. Older. More experienced, he seemed. His voice was calmer than the others.

"I've heard that the New York City District Attorney is investigating the failed bank for selling stock to depositors, with a one year guarantee against loss. What's worse, they didn't honor their promise."

The third voice spoke up. He was the youngest at the table. Despite his graying hair, his voice and body movements were jumping like he was dancing to a jazz band at the Cotton Club instead of talking over a piano rendition of "O, Come, All Ye Faithful."

"Keynes says that the economy is demand-driven. Well, together, government and business spent more in the first half of this year than in the same period last year. I don't think Keynes' theories are panning out."

The man older than the jumpy one refilled everyone's glasses, taking a sip of his as soon as he'd set down the pitcher. Still holding his glass, he motioned to the waiter and pointed to the now-empty pitchers. Then the man began speaking.

"But folks who suffered severe stock market losses last year have cut back their expenditures," argued the second voice. "That's counteracting the boost from government spending, and the severe drought is ravaging the agricultural sector. Food prices are rising."

The third voice was quick to respond.

"That's why banks are dropping interest rates to low levels, but it may backfire on them. The expected deflation and the continuing reluctance of people to borrow signals that consumer spending and investment will be depressed. May's automobile sales declined to below 1928 levels. Prices in general are declining, although wages held steady this year."

The first voice spoke up as I turned back to my table, taking in a good view of the ocean and the cliff before I lifted the napkin from the bread basket. A variety of hard-crusted rolls was inside. I took my time deciding which to try first as I continued to listen to the piano's "Away in a Manger" — once called "Luther's Cradle Hymn," after Martin Luther — and the men's increasingly agitated talk.

"Tell that to the 8,000 shipyard workers who were laid off. Their wages aren't holding steady!"

While that conversation could have had some laughs, the tale was stale.

To the tune of "Silent Night," Mrs. Miller arrived. She wore a sheath dress made of a new lamé fabric that came to market while I was down in Mexico. It was all the rage for evening wear. With its silver metallic threading complemented with sequins and glass beads, Mrs. Miller's dress shimmered even in the candlelight. Her cut-out, T-strap, gray suede pumps had rhinestones in a *fleur-de-lys* design on the top front. At least, they seemed to be rhinestones, and not ice. I stood and held her chair while she took her seat.

"How gallant of you."

"I still have my manners, even if they are rusty."

"We may have to see about blowing the rust out of your pipes."

"We'll get to that. Right now, you should pick your dinner and drinks."

"I like to be surprised. I'll have the chef's special, whatever it is. Let's drink gin and tonics, okay?"

"That sounds good to me."

I gestured to the waiter directly in my line of sight, and he came over. After relaying our choices, I turned to the Miller widow.

"How'd you ditch the kid this afternoon?"

"The kid?"

"The Forty-Niner."

She motioned with her hand like she was sweeping away a fly.

"He's easy to handle. A little sugar goes a long way. Don't worry about him. Let's talk about us."

"And what's with all the flirting with me? I'm old and fat, not in my prime…"

She leaned closer, her jewels and dress glimmering in the candle-light.

"You're not so old and fat that a girl's heart can't feel a flutter from the man you have left inside you."

"That's just the kind of jive I'm talking about. You're still young. You can find a nice young man and start a second family. What gives, Sister?"

My directness must have startled her. She blustered and flustered while I waited for her to spill her side of the story.

"Why, I don't know what you mean."

I waited.

She raised her eyebrows. Then she grimaced.

I waited longer.

She broke off a sprig of holly from the centerpiece, twirled it between her forefinger and thumb, then dropped it onto the evergreen garland. She looked back up at me. She lowered her voice.

"Well, yes, I have been flirting with you, but not to capture you. Not in the way you think. I wanted you to like me…"

"I do."

"I want your help…"

My ears tuned out every sound in the room but her voice. Maybe I'd found my link to the blackmailer. I leaned closer, so she'd feel safe enough to reveal any secrets or indiscretions.

"…and I used the only tool I had: myself. I thought if I could entice you…"

I waited some more. So did she.

"What do you want?" she finally asked.

"What do you want my help with?"

"I want revenge," she blurted, then glanced around the dining room, her fingers covering her lips, to see if anyone had overheard.

Except for the waiter, who seemed too busy pouring our drinks and placing them within reach to eavesdrop, no one seemed to be paying any attention to us.

She turned down the volume.

"I want to hurt the man who cost me my husband."

"Do you mean Paul's cousin, James Crabbe, the one you were taunting at the craps table the other night?"

"Is there any other?"

"Just because he took your husband on a safari?"

"If he hadn't insisted that Paul go to the Kenyan Colony, I'd still have a husband."

"So, let the Forty-Niner rough him up. I bet he'd do anything you asked."

Joanie put down her G&T, and sighed.

"He has a crush, but I seriously doubt if he's capable of violence."

"Shall I give Jimbo the third-degree, or get my gat and knock him off?"

Her shocked voice quavered.

"Heavens, no! I don't want him dead, just hurt."

"He should lose how many limbs?"

"None. He's family. I don't want him disabled, just made sorry for disrupting our lives."

I stayed silent while the waiter returned to put our dinners in front of us. He silently removed the covers and left. Grilled chunks of lobster, shrimp, and calamari lay beside the veal loaf covered with bits of crisp bacon. The vegetable *du jour* was a medley of avocado, *haricots verts,* and caramelized onions. The salad was something I'd heard of but never eaten: a Waldorf salad, with apples, walnuts, raisins. The piano medley continued with "What Child Is This?" The food at Frank's was worth every dollar of the rich client's money. After Mrs. Miller and I had sampled everything on our plates, I returned to our previous discussion.

"Exactly how am I supposed to make Jimbo sorry?"

"Find something on him."

I put down my fork. I wiped my mouth with my napkin to hide my disappointed frown, and regain my composure. I didn't want her — of all the people in the joint — to be part of any blackmail scheme. I didn't want her to be in on any grift. I cleared my throat.

"You want to put the squeeze on Jimbo?"

"What do you mean?"

"You want to get a little bundle in return for Paul's life."

She frowned.

"I don't understand."

"And I can't figure out what you want me to do," I said.

"Nobody in our set is perfect…"

"Neither am I."

"I just want you to get something on him."

"You don't *already* have something?" I said.

"Like what?" she said, her forehead crinkling with another frown.

"Drinking? Gambling?"

"Everybody does that. Including me."

She speared a slice of avocado lying next to the veal loaf and put it into her mouth. I took a drink while waiting for her to chew and swallow her food.

"I just want you to find something that I can let slip out — to a few select people, as a rumor, of course — that will tarnish his reputation."

"Got a good reputation, does he?"

"Not as good as my Paul's," she said, "but good enough."

"What is it, exactly, that you want me to get on Mr. James Crabbe?"

She sighed, fluttering her lashes at me a few times, though clearly not in a flirty-girly way.

"If I knew that, I wouldn't need someone like you, would I?"

I gave her the long look.

"I'm not taking clients right now — I'm retired — but I'll see what I can do for you."

I let her sit for a few minutes before letting her off the hook. She didn't talk to me after we began eating again until I played the gallant, complimenting her attire. Most dames are suckers for approval, and Joanie was no exception.

"That's quite an outfit you're wearing."

"You like it? I wore it just for you."

Her smile radiated warmth.

"Yes, it's nice. Is it that new fabric I read about?"

"Silver lamé! Yes, it is. It also comes in gold, but I think silver goes with my coloring better. How nice of you to notice."

"I notice lots of things. How about you?"

"I notice that you haven't asked me to dance."

"I thought you were only flirting to get my help on settling Jimbo's hash. Since I said I would see what I could do, you don't need bait to fish that pond."

"I wasn't flirting for anything, but a girl needs to dance, and I haven't danced in ages!"

"What will the children think?"

"Let them talk. We can take it."

"There's nothing but Christmas music right now. Maybe later, when the band is playing, we can Foxtrot or something."

"Really?"

"Sure, whatever you like."

Our second pitcher of G&Ts arrived. The waiter poured and left.

"What do you know about the doings here?" I asked.

"What doings?"

"The ones besides gambling, hooch, professional ladies of pleasure, and socialite philandering."

"There are professional ladies of pleasure here?" she asked, looking around the dining room.

"I doubt they leave their rooms on the second floor."

I broke off a sprig of Baby's Breath from the centerpiece. I put half of it in my buttonhole, and the other piece behind her right ear.

"You mean that little girl in blue?"

"What girl in blue?"

"The one who works here."

"Cayte?"

"Is that her name?"

"She cleans my room."

Mrs. Miller shrugged before leaning in toward me.

"Not that I care, of course, but that little girl plays in both camps."

I looked at her.

"She has a sheik *and* a sheba."

"Cayte, the maid."

"If that's her name. The one in blue. From the Casino. The one we saw with the piano player on the beach."

"She's tight with Contina, the piano player."

"She's also tight with one of the other maids. The *other* maid was in the hallway my first day here. I asked for extra hand-towels — I use them to clean off my eye make-up — and that little chippy told *another* maid in the hall to get them from the cart instead of getting them herself..."

"This other maid, the one you saw with Cayte..."

She nodded.

"The one who didn't get me my hand-towels..."

"Did you happen to get *her* name?"

She stared at me as if she didn't understand the question. I didn't pursue it. I let her continue.

"I caught those two girls in a clinch on the stairs the other day. I didn't want to be late for the fashion show, so I took the stairs on the end, like you do. There they were, on the landing, kissing like a house afire. No mistletoe required."

"You don't say."

"I do say. They were quite heated up."

"What did they do when you saw them?" I said, my fingers twirling my glass on the tabletop.

"They broke their clinch, and their flushed faces turned paler than snow, just like that," she said, snapping her fingers. "They apologized for being in my way. I apologized for interrupting them..."

"You apologized?"

"I'm not going to judge people's personal escapades. Though I really think they should do that kind of thing in a room, don't you?"

I looked at her steady.

"She may not look like a lipsticker..."

I had heard a lot of slang, but that was new one on me.

"A what?"

"If girls like other girls *that* way, they're lipstickers. From lipstick, you silly boy, not from kissing. Even though we saw her with the piano player in the Casino and on the beach, she's definitely one of *les girls.*"

"I hear that people get pinched for indiscreet actions."

"Is that little girl in blue getting pinched?"

"She's not rich enough to get squeezed," I said. "She doesn't have enough heavy sugar."

"Like me, you mean?"

I said nothing.

"You think that girl in blue might be trying to squeeze somebody? The piano player, maybe? You want me to keep an eye on her for you?"

"No, the piano player is Frank Torres' nephew. That's a dead angle. As for Cayte, I see her every day when she cleans my room. But if you see the other girl again, you could point her out to me..."

"I'm on it, Boss."

"Or you might at least notice her name."

She gave me a straight look.

I gave it right back.

"But what about you?" I said. "Won't *you* be left open to a grifter, cavorting with a gum-shoe like me?"

"We haven't even danced, let alone done anything that one would need a room for."

She took a long slow drink, her eyes steady on me.

"Still, your social status could suffer."

"I'm not worried about that."

"Perhaps you should. Blackmail is an easy racket."

"I don't do anything to get blackmailed for."

"What about the Forty-Niner?"

She laughed, obviously dismissing him, as well as any scandal involving him.

"If somebody gets leverage, they won't let up until they drain you dry, Sister."

"I don't go to those kind of places."

I gave her the sternest look I could manage.

Her eyes widened.

Eventually.

"That doesn't happen here, does it?"

"It happens everywhere. Nobody is perfect all the time, and when you slip up, there's somebody to take a picture or nab some other incriminating material."

"Why aren't *you* worried about getting pinched?"

I looked her up and down. She did the same to me. It didn't seem like she knew enough about blackmail to even understand who'd be marks and who wouldn't.

I swallowed the last bite of my veal loaf.

"Blackmailers crave money. Big money. I have none. Besides, I have my gat to settle a score if it comes to that. Hasn't any of your social set been scammed?"

"Heavens, no!" she said before she pressed her fingertips to her bare collarbone. "Not that I know of, anyway. Do you want me to try and find out?"

"Don't worry yourself about it, Doll. That's my job."

"Good to know you're on the case."

"But I'm retired," I reminded her.

She nodded, pursing her lips in acquiescence.

Our waiter brought our dessert: *Bûche de Noël.* Jam-filled sponge cake rolled to look like a Yule Log, covered with coffee-buttercream icing, and dotted with blanched almonds, candied cherries, and green-tinted sugar. It was as good as it looked, and, as always, worth every dollar of the client's money.

The conversation flowed like the San Francisco Bay out to the Pacific Ocean. The supper club was as calm and peaceful as bedlam, with a hope that the human flotsam and jetsam would not turn into lagan and be left as derelict for the porters of the Seamen's National Bank.

The Christmas carols stopped when Kid Ory's Creole Orchestra came on and played for hours. In the middle of their third set, they played a few Foxtrots — "Red Roses for a Blue Lady," followed by "Stuff" — so Joanie got her dance.

Several times.

"Painless" was alive and still kicking, but apprehension played with my mind. It was at times like this, when I was enjoying myself — especially with a beautiful, well-dressed, witty woman — that investigations got shot to hell.

Chapter Fifteen

The sun was low in the western sky by the time I parked the Tudor Sedan in front of the office and residence of Edward Marz, M.D., near what used to be the Barbary Coast. The area once was vibrant: every bar and club unique, full of barmaids, ambiance, and dances. The 1914 Red Light Abatement Act was just about as smart as Prohibition: simply hiding vice activities from view. In 1917, the San Francisco Police blockaded the neighborhood and evicted the prostitutes. A dreary sameness settled on the burb, rolled down from City Hall's zoning board. San Francisco's last gas streetlamp was extinguished almost two years ago, on New Year's day, 1929. The brighter electric illumination saved The City just $25Gs a year, but stripped the night scene of color, making everyone's face, even decent citizens', look like mug-shots.

Now those who never ventured outside their homes or churches could sleep better at night knowing that whatever fun and frivolity that had been available there before had gone the way of the dodo. Unfortunately for them, speakeasies sprang up in the empty shells now illuminated by electric street lights. In times of trouble, more people looked for solace in alcoholic spirits than from heavenly ones. The Depression only increased the rate of supplication.

I pressed the door buzzer and waited. After a minute, Dr. Edward Marz opened the door and showed me to the parlor where he saw patients. There were no decorations or any other indication that the doctor was aware of the holiday season. The room behind the plain parlor was a surgery, where he had successfully and discreetly cured me of a few cases of lead poisoning. Upstairs were his living quarters where we had occasionally split a deck of cards and a bottle of whiskey. I sat in one of the two chairs in front of the desk.

"What's bothering you?" he asked.

"I'm short of breath, more than usual. It takes longer each morning to clear my lungs, and lately, I've been coughing up blood."

Dr. Marz waved me into his examining room.

"Take off your shirt and undershirt, and then sit on the examining table."

I did as he asked. He started tapping on my chest. The percussion on my upper-left-side induced me to coughing. Dr. Marz waited while I cleared my lungs.

He pointed to a flat glass panel that stood away from a wall.

"Stand over here, behind the Fluoroscope, facing me."

I complied. When I was in place, he turned off the room light and threw a switch on the wall next to me. There was some buzzing. After a minute, he stood in front of me, but not too close.

"Hmm. Yes, just as I suspected."

He hit the switch behind me, turned on the room light, and then gestured toward the examining table.

"You can get dressed, now."

"What is it, Doc?"

"You have a spot on your lung."

I didn't know what to say, so I kept quiet.

"You're a sick man. The prognosis is not good."

It was just a cough. Those didn't kill you. The Doc gave you something for it, and eventually it went away. Except Dr. Marz was still explaining things to me as I buttoned my shirt.

"You have what may be a lung tumor."

I was at a loss for words. Even my sense of humor had deserted me.

"Last century, lung tumors represented only 1% of all cancers. By 1918, the percentage had risen to almost 10% and just three years ago, they were more than 14%."

I leaned against the examining table. I wanted to take out a smoke, but resisted the urge.

"*The Springer Handbook* that came out this year noted that malignant lung tumors have been increasing since the turn of the century, and accelerated after The Great War."

He looked sympathetic.

"I always thought your job would do you in."

I rubbed that itch on my index finger with my thumb.

"Level with me, Doc. How long do I have?"

"The progress of the disease, from diagnosis until death, is usually from six months to two years."

He put his hand on my shoulder.

"I'm sorry."

"Nothing I can do?" I asked.

"We don't know a lot about it right now. There are some surgical methods — cutting out the tumor — but that seems to just delay the inevitable and then the patient has to recover from the surgery."

"So, no surgery?"

"I don't believe that would help you at this point."

"How did this happen?"

He sighed as he looked up from writing in my chart.

"Some say it is retribution for American decadence, but lung cancer arose at the same rates in countries with fewer automobiles, less industry, and in workers not exposed to benzene or gasoline. The lung cancer rate did not rise after past flu pandemics. The Germans think that smoking may be another possibility, but smoking has been common since the late 17th century."

My head was spinning as if I'd been downing hooch all morning. I was almost unwilling to leave my place at the examining table. I tucked in my shirt as I continued to listen.

"As many investigations failed to show an association between smoking and lung cancer as there were positive findings. But last year, a German doctor, Fritz Lickint, published a paper in which he showed that lung cancer patients were particularly likely to be smokers."

"That won't help me," I said.

Dr. Marz shook his head.

"Not without H. G. Wells' Time Machine to go into the past and warn you off smoking."

"I wouldn't have listened to you anyhow."

I tried to force out a laugh, but it didn't come out right.

"I can't sugarcoat it for you. You can make the most of the time you have. I would suggest moving to an arid climate, which will help your lungs."

"Some place like Mexico?"

"Yes, Mexico will do, but I also suggest that you quit smoking."

"That's not easy."

"If you want a longer life, it is imperative. Try chewing gum: some people say it helps. Now, if you don't have any other questions,

I have another patient coming in. My fee is $5. If you could leave it on the desk on your way out..."

I slipped on my jacket, and dropped a sawbuck on my way out the door.

Outside, the sun was lower than when I'd gone in. I pulled my hope chest out of my inside jacket pocket, shook out one of the cigarettes, lit the Fatima to steady my nerves, and then pointed the Tudor Sedan toward the Bay Point Oyster Company. My next appointment was waiting.

Chapter Sixteen

I parked by the docks, near the loading bay where the oysters came in from the boats. Being late afternoon, the oyster shed was quiet, the day's catch already out at the bars and restaurants for patrons to consume. I walked among the sorting tables, washed down for the next day's catch but still smelling strongly of briny seafood, and into the back of the Bay Point Oyster Company.

Though relatively late in the day, it was early for the late-night supper crowd, so the kitchen was running at half-throttle. I moved past the stations and stoves, everyone too busy at his tasks to pay attention to me. I passed into the restaurant and kept to the left, past the squat Christmas tree trimmed with popcorn-garlands and cut-out snowflakes, toward the bar.

In the third booth, Brian O'Doul held court. I cleared my throat, and he looked up.

"Hey, ya Mug. Are y'alright?"

"Do you have what I want?"

"Right here."

He raised a manila envelope before pointing at the chair opposite him.

"Take a load off. Hey, you're not looking as yourself. Anything ya wanna get offa your chest?"

A waitress wearing a red apron with a pair of green-felt bells sewn on its corner appeared at my elbow as I sat.

"Is the beer still as good as I remember?" I asked.

"As fresh as Humboldt hops in the Fall," she said.

"Fine. Bring me a pint."

"Make that two," O'Doul said. "And we'll be having oysters."

The waitress departed.

He looked at me.

I looked right back.

He figured out quick that I wasn't going to spill anything about myself.

"So, what are you after?"

"I'm looking into some blackmail that's happening at Frank Torres' Roadhouse."

"Torres' Place? You're being serious?"

The waitress came back with our refreshment. After we clicked glasses, we both took long swigs. It was cold and foamy. Just the way I liked it. I wiped the foam from my upper lip with my free hand as I set down the glass.

"You know anything about it?"

"It's a quare aul' world. First I heard of any blackmail at Frank's Place was you telling me just now."

"If you do hear anything — not from me — let me know through the Old Man, will you?"

"Natcherly."

He drained about half his beer without coming up for air. He held his glass up so the waitress could see it. When he looked at me, I nodded. He showed the waitress two fingers.

"I also need to find Joe Kennedy, the boxer."

"Jim Jeffries' old sparring partner?"

"Yeah. He still around?"

"His health took a dive, and he quit the fight game. What're you needing with Joe?"

"Something personal."

"Nothing to do with the blackmail, I'm hoping. 'Cause Joe's not the most inconspicuous fellow, as you may well remember."

The waitress set down two more beers.

"Leave it with me," said O'Doul. "I'll turn Joe up."

"Have him come to the Roadhouse when you do."

The waitress brought some sourdough bread with butter. Neither was as good as the dope they served at Frank's, but it was good enough. I had to be careful: after all, this was just a job, not my life. Any sourdough bread with butter went just fine with *cervezas* and fresh shucked oysters with hot sauce.

O'Doul slipped the file over the tabletop to me.

I put my hand on the file.

"What's the skinny on this?"

"Young Miller died of African Sleeping Sickness."

"That sounds exotic."

"Not quite. It starts with thorns breaking the skin while in the bush. Tsetse flies are attracted to the wound and lay eggs. They hatch, and the larvae carry microscopic parasites that give you the disease."

"No treatment?"

I moved the bread plate aside as the waitress brought out oysters on the half-shell, on piles of ice. O'Doul and I dug in, talking between slurping down the ocean gems.

"It's treatable if seen early enough, but the Miller safari stayed out too long looking for big game."

"Sad way to go," I said, "out in the bush, with a disease eating away at you from the inside."

"To make things worse, Miller had an allergic reaction to Suramin — the drug used to treat it — but he demanded to be full-dosed anyhow."

"The Miller widow said her husband was brave, and that he took risks that no one else would take. He was probably betting that he was lucky enough to take the medicine."

"He was all in on losing that bet. The Sumarin or the allergic reaction or both, they damaged his kidneys, which failed on the boat back to the States."

"What a mess."

We both drank some more beer and had some more oysters. We spent another hour and more beers catching up on our parts of world events. After that, I made ready to leave.

"Aye. It's time you put a hole in it. The road's already dark. If you leave now, you might make the Roadhouse by midnight."

"Put this on the Old Man's Account. Our client's got the jake to pay the freight."

I tipped my Fedora and left. Outside, out of habit, I glanced around before I went to my car. No one else was around.

I opened the car door and laid the folder on the seat. I didn't know how I could help the Miller widow out with any of the information I'd gotten so far, since it all seemed to be on the up and up, leaving Cousin Jimbo in the clear.

Once inside the car, I drove circumspectly north, before turning south toward Frank's Roadhouse. I wondered if "Spider" Aures was waiting for me somewhere on the road.

Train at Moss Beach Station (Historic Photo)

Frank's Place Roadside Sign
(Historic Photo)

Frank's Place (Roadhouse)
with Vintage (contemporaneous) Cars
(Historic Photo)

Frank's Place (Roadhouse), **with** *The Marine View Motel*
and the Montara Beach Hotel, Cliff View
(Historic Photo)

Frank's Place, Dining Room
with view of Ocean & Bluff
(Historic Photo)

Frank's Roadhouse Dining Room,
Decorated for Special Event
(Historic Photo)

*Frank's Roadhouse, with garage for
bootleg liquor in lower left (Historic Photo)*

*Moss Beach Distillery, formerly Frank's Place (Roadhouse),
Aerial View showing rear of MBD, path, bluff, beach, ocean*

Chapter Seventeen

*I*t was mid-morning at the Roadhouse. My morning coughing fit was over, so I drank a cup of java. Cayte was just starting on cleaning my room, and I was observing the parking lot from my window. A car swerved into the parking lot and, brakes squealing, came to a stop.

Cayte came up behind me as the man got out. Her sharp intake of breath made me look at her. She was more afraid than any woman had a right to be.

"Don't let him find me!" she whispered.

"Who?"

She pointed to the new arrival.

"My husband."

I stood and walked her away from the window, deeper into my room.

"Stay in here, and keep the door closed. He won't find you. You'll be fine."

I patted her hand.

"I'll go see what's up."

"Be careful!"

I showed her my gun.

"Here's my *Careful.*"

I went to the breezeway, where I heard noises in the club. The husband was having words with Contina. They had just got to the fighting part when I arrived. I broke them apart.

"Take it outside!"

They did: into the parking lot. I figured I'd done my job. What they did to each other outside the Roadhouse didn't concern me. As long as neither of them had a weapon. Though the husband was broader and taller than the Piano-man, the fight was a real barn-burner. Contina was tough, and didn't seem to mind messing up his hands.

"Are you banging my wife?" the husband yelled at Contina, landing several body blows.

"That's none of your business," Contina replied.

The husband was a brawler, all right: all weight and no skill. He was slow and predictable. Contina, on the other hand, ducked and swayed like he was experienced in more than just street-fights. He was a counter-puncher, waiting till the bigger opponent swung — mostly wild — before he blocked or slipped past them. And Contina had a chin, absorbing the big punches while still standing. The husband tried to complement his hits below the belt with vicious talk.

"She's got a taste for girls, you know."

Contina feinted with his left, then threw a straight right, landing one in the center of the husband's chest, but the big guy didn't flounder. Even with a mouse swelling on his forehead over his left eye, the husband just kept on leading with his chin, one of the most vulnerable spots. It was beginning to look like he'd never had a bout with anyone but a woman.

"You know she's a lesbian, don't you?"

"I know how to satisfy a dame," shouted Contina between his opponent's wild punches, "even if you don't."

"Why, I oughta beat up you *and* her girlfriend both."

"Any guy who'd use his own wife as a punching bag doesn't scare me."

The husband was worse than a Palooka. He was nothing but a bully. A Tomato Can, bleeding from his nose, lip, and the swelling over his eye. Then he tried to Rabbit Punch the back of Contina's head and neck — illegal in any ring, and unethical even on the streets — and as Contina swung to avoid the danger, the bully took a punch at Contina, slamming him square in the mouth, splitting his lower lip. Just as the Piano-man got some decent jabs in, a few of Torres' goons poured out of the Roadhouse like a murderous, black-suited river. Cayte's husband saw them coming, and threw a last, wild Haymaker. He broke away, running for his car, saved by the metaphorical bell.

"This ain't over, Contina!" he yelled out his open car window as he left the lot, turning toward The City.

The goons talked to the Piano-man, probably asking if he wanted them to go after the guy, but the kid was the real thing. He shook his head, wiped the blood from his split-lip with his handkerchief, combed back his hair with his fingers, tucked in his wrinkled and bloodied shirt, and walked steady back to the Roadhouse. I followed the group.

I was about to return to my room to give Cayte the *all clear,* when the desk clerk called to me.

"There was a call for you. He left a message."

I read the note as I climbed the stairs. Joe Kennedy was at a motel in San Bruno, a little town south of San Francisco. I unlocked the door to my room.

"Cayte, I'm alone and coming in."

She came out of the bathroom.

"I heard him yelling when he was driving away. He didn't get hurt bad, did he?"

"Your husband and Contina fought it out until Torres' goon squad arrived. Your husband must not have liked those odds, so he hopped into his flivver and took out north."

"I'm glad nobody was hurt bad. My husband has to take care of our little boy. At least until I can get some other arrangements made. And Johnny... Mr. Contina..."

I looked at her until she stopped talking.

"I have an errand to run," I said. "I don't think your husband will be back. At least not today. You'll be okay here, right?"

"Yes, sir."

"Good."

I picked up my hat and left, thinking about what the Miller widow had said she'd seen in the stairwell between Cayte and the other — as yet unidentified — maid.

I went down the stairs wondering why a pretty girl like Cayte needed even more complications in her life than a husband *and* a boyfriend could provide.

Chapter Eighteen

I left the El Camino Real after passing through Millbrae, and pulled the jalopy to the curb outside the Shady Grove Motel. San Bruno had been a city for sixteen years, but still looked like the ranch land it came from. Down the road, I could see the Tanforan horse racing track, closed since California's do-gooders decided in 1911 to outlaw gambling. That was as wrong as Prohibition.

Our rich client's deceased husband, Adolph Spreckels, raised thoroughbreds on his farm in Napa, and his colt Morvich won the Kentucky Derby in '22. A Spreckels syndicate reopened the track — *sans* wagering — for seasons '23 and '24. The track closed with Spreckels' death in 1924, which was attributed to pneumonia, because the social elite did not die from advanced stage syphilis. It must have been in a latent stage when he and the younger Alma de Bretteville had married and had their family since she showed no signs of the disease, and had still seemed healthy and vital when she'd approved me in the restaurant with the Chief.

I found Joe Kennedy in room 110. I knocked. After a minute, the door opened.

"Heya, Mug," I said. "How've you been?"

Kennedy stepped back, holding the door open as wide as the big grin on his puss beneath his permanently flattened nose.

"I've seen better days."

He gestured to the thread-bare couch, taking the worn-out armchair for himself. There was no sign in his place that he was planning any Christmas celebrations, not even for himself. Beyond the simple living room area was a bed with an obviously saggy mattress, and a scratched-up dresser; beyond that, a bathroom. I hoped that his rent was as cheap as the décor.

"So, what can I do you for?" he asked.

"I need some help on a job."

"I'm listening."

"I need a man tailed and spoken to about his antics."

"What's he been up to?"

"He's a wife-beater, and is causing trouble with one of the maids at the hotel I'm working for the Old Man."

Kennedy leaned back in his armchair, frowning, and put his bare feet up on the threadbare ottoman in front of him.

"I thought the Old Man disapproved of getting involved in domestic disputes."

"I need the maid's eyes and ears for a case I'm working."

"I thought you retired."

"I get that a lot. You interested?"

He nodded.

"Since I have nothing on my plate, I'll sign on."

"I appreciate that," I said, standing.

"How do you want me to take care of him after I tail him?"

"Just scare him off for a while."

When Kennedy pulled himself out of the chair and stood, I gave him the once-over.

"You look thin. Are you okay?"

"The doc's running tests; he don't know what it is."

"There's a lot of that going around these days."

"So, what's the pay?" he asked.

"I can pay you the Agency's daily rate for stringers, and front you a few weeks' pay with car fare."

"That's jake."

I peeled two Jacksons off my bill roll.

"This will get you started. I'm at Torres' Roadhouse in Half Moon Bay. When you come down, it's okay to know me, but keep it on the Q-T."

"Gotcha."

After he got a couple of beers from the fridge, we caught up on old times and the fight game, from which Kennedy's health had forced him out. At 6 foot 2 and 220 pounds, he was still moxie enough to mix it up with street fighters. Since Cayte's husband wasn't even talented enough to win a street-fight, I wasn't too worried about Kennedy handling the job that I was passing to him.

Kennedy told me about a guy playing for the San Francisco Seals, a Vince DiMaggio, insisting that I had to see Vince's kid brother Joe, who was going to be a baseball phenomenon.

We said our goodbyes, and I left. A car followed me for a few miles, but after a few turns, I lost him. I began to wonder if any more surprises would be waiting for me around the next bend.

Chapter Nineteen

*I*n the morning, Cayte was just coming into the room to clean when I stopped her.

"Come on, show me the rooms that hardly ever need cleaning."

"Do you mean the one that only needs bedding, and the other one that only needs the ashtrays emptied?"

"Yes, those ones."

She looked uneasy as she glanced back over her shoulder at my bed and bathroom.

"Don't worry," I said. "I'll take any heat over the condition of this room if anybody sees it before you get back."

We locked the door behind us, pushing the cleaning cart against the wall in the hallway before I followed her down the hall to a set of rooms just past the middle stairs. Being mid-morning in the middle of the week, the corridor was empty, except for us.

"These are the ones I told you about. The first one is the ashtray room."

She pointed to the next room just next down the hall.

"That's the room that sometimes needs a bed change and clean towels in the bathroom."

"What about the one where you think there's a poker marathon? The one that needs all the extra glasses, and lots of extra towels in the bathroom?"

"That's this one, the ashtray room."

I reached over, took her master key from her apron pocket, and unlocked both doors. She looked worried.

"It's okay: Frank Torres and I go way back."

I unlocked both rooms.

"Okay, but please don't do anything that will get me or my roommate in trouble."

"I'll be as quiet and unobtrusive as a church mouse. I won't even leave any crumbs."

I dangled the master key in front of her until she took it.

"You can go make up my room."

As she walked away I slipped into the sometimes-dirty-bed room to see the floor-plan.

There was a small living room in the front and the one bedroom in the back, with a window facing the ocean bluff. In between the two rooms was the bathroom. The place was cleaner than clean. It hadn't seen action of any kind lately. Once I'd scoped out the floor-plan, I left to go into the ashtray room.

Just then, the supper club's hat check girl was coming up the stairs. I pressed back into the sweaty-linen room and drew the door closed. I stood to the side of the doorframe, in case this room was her destination. I heard her pass the room, walking toward the cathouse at the end of the hallway.

After she was far enough down the corridor, I left the sweaty-linen room, and entered the dirty-ashtray room next to it.

It was the mirror image of the other hotel room. I searched the wall of the living room and found a false panel separating the living room and the bathroom next door. The panel was painted to match the lathe and plaster walls. I slid it to the right an inch and then could lift it up, where a slight twist allowed it to be removed.

Inside the hollow wall space was a Leica camera mounted in a rack that held the camera lens tight against the wall facing the sometimes-dirty-bedroom next door. It was probably set to a fixed focal length with fast film to allow pictures to be taken in low light. There was no film in the camera. This set-up would have to be activated by someone just before the "evidence" was captured.

I replaced the panel and gave the rest of the hotel room a close examination. The bathroom had no secret panels I could find, but it did contain a peephole for a camera lens.

The bedroom was another story. There were two cameras hidden in the wall facing the bedroom next door, and in the ceiling was a panel that had a camera mounted to a periscope that looked down on the bed next door. This set-up would also have to be activated by someone just before the "evidence" was captured. None of the cameras had film in them. I replaced the panels.

Just before I left the room, I turned and examined it again. Something wasn't right. Something besides the hidden cameras. It only took me a minute or two to figure out what was missing: the

Poinsettias. I returned to the first room. Same situation there. Not even the nominal seasonal decoration in either room.

I met no one in the hallway as I strolled back in my own room, where I found Cayte finishing up. She looked frightened as I made myself a Rye and soda, and smoked a few Fatimas.

"Everything all right?" she said.

I nodded.

"Those rooms are clean, by the way, so you won't have to do anything to them today."

She nodded and went back to my bathroom with clean towels. When Cayte was ready to leave, I stopped her.

"Where does your husband live?"

"Why? What are you going to do?"

"I'm not going to do anything. But I have somebody who could talk to him. He may listen to reason."

"Do you think so?"

"My fellow talks a good game."

She seemed doubtful, but she gave me her previous address anyway.

"2270 Folsom Street in the Mission District, near the fire station."

"That's a house?"

"Apartment 23."

I wrote it all down on the back of one of my cards.

"I'll have my guy talk some sense into him."

She looked doubtful.

"Don't hurt him."

"I wouldn't think of it."

"He has to take care of our boy till I get him with me."

"I remember that part of the story."

I gestured toward the hallway.

"You can lock up those other rooms now."

After she left, I left too, and walked to the breezeway office. I asked the clerk for some gum. If he was surprised, he didn't let it show. I bought a few packs of Beeman's to try instead of smoking so many Fatimas.

Working the gum over between my cheek and jaw, I went to the phone booth in the lobby and had the hotel operator ring up Shady Grove Motel in San Bruno. Joe Kennedy didn't answer in his room. I repeated the address that Cayte had given me in a message for him with the hotel operator. Then I tore up the card with the information written on it and deposited the fragments into one of the lobby receptacles.

That business taken care of, I turned toward the supper club, looking for trouble before it found me.

Chapter Twenty

*I*t was dark outside, and I was having after dinner cocktails with Mrs. Miller. Cayte was off-duty and wearing her blue gown, sitting with Contina at a table to the bluff side of the room. They had drinks but no food. I was keeping an eye on them, but Mrs. Miller was more interested in something else.

"I'm just surprised," the widow opined, "that with all of the shenanigans the Social Register pulls here, I haven't heard of any blackmail going on."

"Maybe we just don't know about it. After all, for blackmail to work, it has to be hidden from the public."

"Then how are we going to be able to toss the crooks from the party?"

"The blackmailers are set up for the pinch," I said, shutting up just as the waiter arrived with our food.

After we admired the presentation of the roasted squab and the lobster salad, we got to work.

"Blackmailers have to collect incriminating evidence of the embarrassing deed, and then later, show it to the target."

"So, after they get the goods, they go after the jack."

"You do need some damaging evidence before you can try to get any dough to keep it hushed up."

She nibbled some of the sugar off the rim of her glass. Then she flashed her pearly whites at me.

"Nerts!" she practically squealed, snapping her fingers.

"You just thought of something good?"

"We could start flirting — hitting on all sixes — do some serious cuddling in public, and then see who tries to snap our picture."

I shook my head.

She frowned.

"That's too direct. Blackmailers are shy…"

"Shy?"

"They avoid any situations that they didn't set up themselves."

"So I can't get caught with you *in flagrante?*"

She put a pout on display.

"Pouts quit working on me a long time ago."

I noticed movement near the entrance. It was Cayte's husband searching the room with his eyes.

"Excuse me," I said to Mrs. Miller.

I stood and went to the entrance, taking the side route opposite where Contina and Cayte were. I waved my hand to get the husband's attention. He looked at me hard, probably trying to work out who I was and what I would want with him.

My ruse worked. Before he returned to his scanning, Cayte had left the table where the couple had been sitting, and ducked into an alcove.

The husband espied Contina, though. I arrived at the table just as the re-match was getting started. I moved them outside through one of the bluff-side French doors.

"I don't know what you want with me," Contina said. "I didn't take her away from you."

Cayte stood outside.

"Stop this fighting!"

"Stop?" her husband said. "I'm just getting started. You're going to come home with me or else."

Cayte looked to Contina, who shrugged. She took off running around the breezeway office and then along the bluff. Her husband followed, gaining ground with each step.

I looked at Contina.

"She doesn't want me permanent, so it's not my problem," he said. "She's too much trouble anyway."

I took off after the couple, doing the best I could to catch them. The moon was in the waxing gibbons phase, and I could just about see their faces as the husband caught her. I had to stop for a few seconds to catch my breath and to let the coughing stop. I spit something dark on the ground and went toward them again. The bully shook Cayte and then threw her to the turf, her hat falling off. As she tried to rise, her right heel sank into the sand, dropping her down on one knee and hand, her body leaning slightly away from her husband. Before she could get her balance, he grabbed her by the hair. She shrieked, slapping at him as he dragged her up.

I forced my legs and lungs to work harder. He obviously meant business, and I intended to shut him down if Contina couldn't carry the weight. He slapped her a few times, keeping her on her feet by holding the front of her dress. The guy really needed to be hurt by that time. Cayte kicked his shins, and pounded his chest, but she was a dame up against a heavyweight. She didn't have a chance. I cursed Contina for not being a real man. I cursed my old and fat body for being too slow.

Cayte's husband acted like he was in the ring. He right-arm jabbed at her body several times, connecting with her abdomen, her ribs, her chest. She screamed. Louder than if he'd just punched her. In the moonlight, the front of her dress darkened. It looked like he was holding something in his hand. A pocket-knife. No wonder she'd screamed so loud. I ran harder. He shoved her backwards, away from him.

She stumbled, lost her balance, and tumbled over the bluff.

I cursed my old, fat body again. Now the husband heard or saw me coming, and took off running around the hotel building, making for the parking lot. Short of breath, I arrived at the bluff. Cayte was down there. I looked for a way to rescue her, but saw none. Leaning out, I could see her broken body on the rocks below.

I knew it was a long shot, but I turned to chase the husband. As I rounded the building to arrive at the edge of the parking lot, I saw him get into a truck. Before I went another twenty feet, he was speeding away.

Leaning onto a car, I coughed up blood in spittle until I was dizzy.

Chapter Twenty-One

*I*n the morning, the San Mateo County Sheriff was out with his crew, retrieving Cayte's body from the beach.

I had the hotel operator put through a call to Joe Kennedy. I was in luck, and he picked up the phone in his room. After the operators had clicked off the line, I gave Joe the news about Cayte.

"I'll take care of this," he responded.

"Good."

I hung the phone in its cradle. I skipped breakfast and poured myself a double Rye.

After the Sheriff's posse left, it didn't stay quiet for long. Unmarked cars with sirens blaring shot by the Roadhouse, heading south toward Año Nuevo Point.

I grabbed my hat, locked the room, and went downstairs to the breezeway. A few minutes later, Frank Torres came out of the office with a flock of his black-suited crows. The foot soldiers fanned out to their cars. Torres made toward his big touring car. I followed him. He turned to me.

"What do you want?"

"It looks like some action. Can I tag along?"

"Sure, why not? Maybe you can catch a bullet for me."

"Except I didn't bring my mitt."

I got into the back seat while he took the wheel. Contina came out and climbed into the front seat with Torres. Contina's jaw was bruised.

"The Prohibition Cops are raiding the wharf in Pescadero," Torres said. "We won't step in until it's over. If they get anything, we'll hijack the truck and take the booze."

"Won't the Santa Cruz mob want their liquor back?" Contina asked.

"If they lose it and we recover it, who can say that we didn't own it in the first place?"

"What's your plan?" I asked.

"About five miles north of Pescadero Beach, just after San Gregorio Road, the coast highway bends a half mile inland before bending back north. We'll set up there with a group of men to take the Prohibition police's truck if it comes to that. The rest of my men went to Pescadero to fight the cops from the north while the Santa Cruz mob fights them from the south. We'll teach the Feds to not interfere with supply and demand!"

"This should be fun," I said.

We were heading south, and the road made a gentle turn to the East before executing a sharp turn to the right. We came around so we were heading west, even pointing a little north, before swinging back to a southwest run.

At San Gregorio Road, Torres pulled off and stopped behind two cars full of his men. He got out for a chat. Returning to our touring car, he pulled across the highway, heading back to the hairpin turn.

"It's all set. When the Prohibition Cops pass them, they'll pull in behind. We'll be waiting around the first bend, with our car pulled across the road. They'll stop and we'll take the truck."

"If it were that easy, everyone would be doing it," I said.

"Discussion time is over now."

Torres stopped the car and then backed it to block the highway. We got out and stood behind the car, facing the northbound traffic when it came. Fortunately, there wasn't much traffic in these rural stretches of highway.

We didn't wait long before gunfire could be heard in the distance. After a moment, a big truck came around the bend, with five or six sedans chasing it. Our car was blocking the highway. The driver of the truck slammed on his brakes. Two of the chase cars came around the truck and blocked the shoulders of the road on either side. The remaining cars blocked the rear.

Gunfire raged, the staccato snapping sounds of handguns mixed with the larger blasts of sawed-off shotguns. One of Torres' hoods tossed a small grenade into the cab of the truck. The explosion took out the front windshield. I couldn't see it, but the gunfight in the rear of the truck ended, too. I never fired a shot.

One of Torres' men hopped into the cab of the truck. After dumping the dead bodies on the side of the road, we made a convoy heading north. Before we got to Moss Beach, the truck and three cars took the dirt road that went over the hill to San Mateo.

"Where are they going?" I asked.

"I like you a lot," Torres answered, "but not well enough to tell you my business."

"After all we've been through?"

"Especially that. You taking our side today stood you in good stead with me. Just don't press your luck."

"At least I wasn't bored sitting at the Roadhouse."

I was getting pretty chummy with Torres, but I still didn't trust him not to kill me.

Not if a good reason and the opportunity presented itself.

Chapter Twenty-Two

*W*hen I returned to the Roadhouse, a message was waiting for me at the front desk. It was from Joe Kennedy. I called his motel from the lobby phone booth and asked the clerk to ring his room. Joe got straight to it.

"It's finished."

"What happened?"

"The Doc says I've got stomach cancer, the incurable kind."

"I'm sorry to hear that."

Joe made an noise that could have meant a lot of things. I waited for him to tell me the rest of his story.

"Later that day, when I saw the wife-beater you wanted to get a message to, and he said he didn't mean to hurt her that bad, I snapped. When I stopped, he was for the worms."

"Are you okay?"

"I'm not feeling great, but I didn't mean to be a Torpedo…"

"You need some extra dough to get out of town?"

"No, I didn't leave any traces…"

I reached for the Fatimas. I stopped myself. Joe was still talking.

"…Not that it matters now," he was saying. "I only got a few weeks, the Doc says."

"That's rough."

"Ain't as rough as being permanent punch-drunk, I guess."

"I suppose each of us has his own definition of 'rough'," I said.

Joe didn't respond.

"I'll have your money delivered to your motel. You sure you don't want some extra? You could go someplace. Mexico's nice."

"Too tired to go anywhere."

"Sorry, Joe."

"Me, too. Hey, take care of yourself, you Mug."

"Yeah, you, too."

I exited the phone booth into the lobby. Two men in navy blue suits stood at the counter. That was my first clue that they didn't work at the Roadhouse.

"We're Prohibition Agents. Get your boss down here, pronto."

"Front."

The clerk signaled, and a bellhop came to the counter.

"Please find Mr. Torres and let him know that two Officials are here requesting to see him," the desk clerk said to the bellhop. "Gentlemen, if you would please take advantage of the chairs over there."

He indicated the plush seats to the side of the reception area.

"No, thanks. We'll stand here."

Prohibition Agents are undisciplined and unprincipled men who create havoc by using all forms of harassment, entrapment, and abuse to make arrests. Grabbing victims was their job. Getting convictions was for the District Attorney to worry about.

I stood by the phone booth, checking my watch, admiring the Christmas tree decorations.

After a few minutes, Torres came down the stairs and strode to the two agents.

"I'm Frank Torres. What can I do for you gentlemen?"

"We're here from Earl Warren's office. We'd like to ask you a few questions."

"Seeing how Mr. Warren is the District Attorney of Alameda County, but we're in San Mateo County, he lacks jurisdiction. I see no reason why I should talk to you."

"Our badges are backed by the Hatch Act. We are merely working with D.A. Warren as a local liaison."

"He's hardly local. The East Bay is two counties away from here. It sounds like the young hot-shot Warren is bucking for enough juice to make a play for Attorney General. Who knows: maybe he wants to be the Governor of California?"

"We wouldn't know about that. We're here on a routine matter."

"And what would that be?"

"There was a raid down near Año Nuevo. One of the liquor trucks went missing. D.A. Warren is the head of a task force against illegal alcohol in northern California, so he asked us to look into the matter."

"This is the first I've heard of any raid or a truck that went missing. Perhaps one or more of your fellow agents knows more than he's saying."

"Perhaps one or more of your men is moonlighting," the second agent said.

"I don't know what my employees do in their free time. I have a business to run, and that takes all my energy."

They tried to stare something more out of Torres, but he just stood there until they started to clear their throats. Without changing the expression on his face, Torres made a suggestion.

"How about if you do your investigating, and I'll do mine?"

The taller one narrowed his eyes at Torres, who casually turned away, motioning the desk manager toward him.

"If we need to continue this conversation, we can talk through my lawyers," said Torres, taking the stack of mail the manager offered him. "I believe we're done here, Gentlemen."

"Hardly," said the second agent without moving an inch.

"Not by a long shot," said the first, standing up straighter and pushing his chest out.

Torres turned and climbed the stairs, shuffling through the pile of envelopes as he went, leaving the two Prohibition Agents standing there. The second agent looked over at me.

"What are you gawking at?" he said.

"Nothing a nice stiff drink wouldn't make me forget," I said.

He took a step toward me. His partner put his hand on the second agent's arm.

"Don't," the first agent said.

"I don't like his attitude," said the second.

"So we'll pick him up along with the rest of Torres' mob when the time comes."

"Only I'm not with Torres," I said.

"What's your angle here?" the first one asked.

"I used to be a private detective. I'm taking a little holiday before retiring to Tijuana. I won't be here when you come back."

"Just make that the truth," said the one with the attitude, pointing his forefinger at me, "and we'll have no problems."

I gave him my most unconcerned expression. The manager pretended to be busy doing something behind the desk, but he was watching us. The first agent nudged the second, then made a slight jerk with his head. The second one frowned, but turned away.

They left together.

My stomach growled. I was hungry. Besides, I had my job to do. The restaurant was a good place to listen for clues.

Chapter Twenty-Three

I was having luncheon when George Whittell, Jr. entered. He was a notorious playboy who lived a pell-mell life full of beautiful women, luxury boats, and automobiles. He took $50M out of the Stock Market just before The Crash.

The cigarette girl stopped at Whittell's table and proffered her wares. From the way she bent forward he could see her well-stocked inventory alongside the bright sprig of holly. He selected three Cuban cigars and a pack of Lucky Strikes, and then tipped her well. Before she left, she whispered something in his ear. He smiled at her as she straightened, turned her backside toward him and then sashayed away. He admired that view as well.

It seemed that several of the women who worked at the Roadhouse made excuses to stop by Whittell's table to display their holiday garnish. It was a wonder that he had time to eat. Eventually, he stood and went toward the Casino. Having already signed my check, I followed.

We took the stairs at the rear of the club which led up and back to a wrought iron grate bolted onto a red-stained wooden door. Whittell looked at me. I gestured toward the door. He tapped on the panel.

It slid open.

"Yeah?"

"Diamond Jim sent me," Whittell said.

The panel closed, and I could hear the sound of a bolt being drawn.

Whittell looked to me.

"I guess they found the oil can."

"About time they lubed those hinges," I replied.

The thick wooden door opened onto the unadorned vestibule with another door on the opposite wall.

"Welcome."

After the doorman waved us inside, he closed and bolted the door.

"You both are familiar to me."

"We know the routine," I said.

"Is Anna Philbrick here?" Whittell asked.

"I've not seen her yet today. Perhaps she will be in later."

The doorman opened the second door and waved us in. The door swung shut.

Whittell went to the closest Blackjack table.

Edward Ory was there, drinking at the bar. I joined him.

"Don't you know that you're not supposed to drink alone?" I asked.

"Then join me," he replied. "I'm just getting loose for tonight."

"Do you know an Anna Philbrick?"

"Yeah, she's Contina's woman, only she takes other sheiks on the side. Shebas, too, I hear..."

"Shebas?"

"Yeah. Why?"

"Just putting a name I heard somewhere in the proper place on the scorecard."

He finished his Southside and ordered another. He looked over to the Blackjack table.

"You came in with George Whittell. Social climbing?"

"Too rich for my blood."

"That reminds me: have you been avoiding our poker games?"

"I've been busy. I'll stop by tonight, if I can."

"You do that. I need to visit my money and invite it to come home."

The Miller widow entered the Casino, wearing a slinky, black, sleeveless dress with the neckline cut in a deep V, front and back. She was wearing the string of perfectly matched pearls — wrapped once around her neck so that the diamond-studded clasp showed just above the hollow between her collarbones — then falling down the front, knotted once just below her waist, their movement emphasizing the sway of her hips. Her wavy hair was pulled back into a chignon at the nape of her neck, so that the diamond-topped pearl earrings that matched the necklace were also visible. Her eyebrows, eyes, and lips were all done to perfection. When she noticed me, she walked over. Greta Garbo and Marlene Dietrich had nothing that Mrs. Miller didn't have.

"I'll see you later," I said to Ory.

He grinned.

"Don't get too busy and miss our poker game."

I went to greet Mrs. Miller. She ordered a French-75, took a sip of the imitation gin-champagne, and then looked me in the eyes.

"Where have you been? I haven't seen you in days."

"I had some matters to attend to, that's all. Have you kept yourself busy?"

"I had a terrible scare while you were away."

"Did you find out something for me?"

She shook her head.

She looked around behind her, over her shoulder, while I waited. When she leaned closer, she whispered.

"I saw her."

"Who?"

"That girl."

I looked at her without betraying any expression.

"The one in blue. From on the beach."

"You mean Cayte?"

She nodded.

"You told me that already. Did you get that other maid's name?"

She put her fingers on the back of my wrist, preventing me from picking up my Scotch and soda.

"I mean, I saw the girl in blue while you were gone."

"But her husband killed her."

"I know that," she said, motioning the bartender for another French-75.

I stayed quiet.

"I saw her in the hallway, outside my room," she continued. "I saw her out of the corner of my eye, but I know it was the same girl. I recognized the dress. She wore it whenever she wasn't working."

I drained my glass and moved it closer to the bartender, who was just delivering Mrs. Miller's next *faux* champagne. He pointed to my empty glass and gave me a questioning look. I nodded my agreement to another.

She gripped my hand under the railing of the bar. It seemed to calm her a bit, so I let her hold my paw. After the next round of drinks arrived, she downed hers straight away.

"Take it easy there. You don't want to end the evening before it's even started, do you?"

"I've had the heebie-jeebies ever since I saw her..."

"Cayte's dead. You do know that, right?"

"Why do you think I was so scared? Why do you think I was looking for you?"

She gave me a wide-eyed look. She wasn't playing me. She really seemed to think that she'd seen the maid.

I let her squeeze my hand as tightly as she wanted, for as long as she needed. I pushed the next drink slightly away from her. I needed to hear the rest of the story. She took a few deep breaths. Gradually, she relaxed her grip on my hand. Just having me there seemed to make her feel safer. She took a deep breath. And another drink.

"One of my earrings went missing, too."

"Which ones?"

"Just one... one of these."

She pointed to her right ear.

"But you're wearing them."

"Yes, I know. I'm telling you that one earing was gone, but then it showed up."

She swallowed down another drink. She must have still been pretty upset. I'd never seen her trying to get tight before.

"Do you think one of the maids nicked your pearl earrings?"

"Just one earring. The other one was still on the dresser next to my jewel box."

"You're sure they weren't both there? Mixed up with the necklace maybe?"

She shook her head.

"They're in separate velvet bags. I took the earrings out one night, to wear them for dinner, and after I'd fastened my dress and went back to the dresser, one of the pearls was gone."

"Did you tell the manager?"

She shook her head.

"Why not?"

"Later, the missing earring was back. Only it was next to the bathroom sink."

"You didn't carry it in there yourself?"

"I never take jewelry into the bathroom. If I dropped it, it might go down the drain."

"So, one of your pearl earrings disappeared for a while, but then it was back."

"Yes. It gives me the heebie-jeebies."

Edward Ory stood and made to leave, giving me a high sign. I smiled and shook my head in the affirmative. Before Joanie noticed my divided attention, I spoke to her fears.

"A maid must have moved it while she was cleaning."

"No, the earring went missing when I was alone in the room. I took the earrings out of the velvet bag, and then before I went to put them on, one of them was gone."

She gave me a look I'd never seen on her face before.

"Do you believe in ghosts?"

"I'm a Detective: we live by deductive reasoning and what we can prove. Ghosts aren't in either of those categories."

"But I saw her. And my earring…"

I patted her hand and used my most reassuring voice.

"If Cayte's haunting the Roadhouse, they couldn't have gotten a sweeter ghost."

Mrs. Miller visibly relaxed. All of the drinks may have helped, too. I gave her a few more minutes to calm down.

"Do you know Anna Philbrick?" I asked. "She works here somewhere."

"No. Why?"

"Nothing really. I've just heard her name myself. How about George Whittell?"

She nodded slightly toward the Blackjack table, and then raised one of her finely outlined eyebrows.

"I know which one he is," I said. "We came in at the same time."

"Then why'd you ask who he was?"

"I asked what you *knew* about him."

Mrs. Miller sighed.

"I'm all at loose ends when you're away, it seems," she said. "I've forgotten how to be a good stoolie."

She picked up her drink and turned casually toward the players in the room, keeping her voice low.

"By reputation, Whittell's a wild one."

"Wild?"

"Cavalier, as they say."

"Now, there's a playmate for you," I said.

"Are you trying to get rid of me?"

"Not at all. But you're not going to be permanently interested in an old, fat man like me."

"I'm not interested in a playboy like George Whittell either," she said. "Besides, he wouldn't be interested in me."

I gave her my best look of surprise.

"You're a gorgeous woman."

"I'm the widow of an exciting, *faithful* man."

"Maybe you're the type he's been looking for."

"Thank you for the vote of confidence, but he's already pinched two different elves' *derrières* in the past couple of minutes, and tried to stroke another's sprig of holly."

She'd slowed her drinking, which must have meant her heebie-jeebies weren't in flower any longer. She stopped observing Whittell, and looked at me.

"What gives with you tonight?" she said. "Are you trying to pawn me off?"

"I didn't know that you were mine to pawn."

"Keep it up and you'll be sleeping alone tonight."

"That sounds like an invitation that was canceled before it was sent," I said.

"You're about as bright as night."

"I know how to turn on the lights: you just finger the little switch."

"Maybe you can show me how you do that."

"Maybe I can, but right now, I need to visit the proprietor of this establishment..."

Before Mrs. Miller could protest, I continued.

"Maybe you could play some Blackjack. Make like Simon Templar *and* Sherlock Holmes."

"Really?"

She looked pleased.

"Get a wiggle on, Doll. See what you can learn."

She stood, smoothing her dress over her hips, touching her hair, and picking up her drink. She turned to me.

"You look perfect."

"Thanks, Boss."

"Now go try and get the goods."

"Just on Whittell, or on anybody?"

"Whittell, primarily, but I'll take whatever you give me."

"Promises, promises," she said, giving me a wink before she strolled over to the table.

I took my leave of the young widow, and made my way out the back and down to the lobby.

"Is Mr. Torres busy?" I asked the desk clerk.

"Mr. Torres is not here today. Would you like to leave a message?"

"That's okay. I can see him some other time."

I turned to explore what other options I had.

Chapter Twenty-Four

I went into the supper club and asked to be seated at a small side table. It was still early afternoon, so I ordered cocktails for two. I had a lot to think about. Joanie was convinced that she had seen a ghost. I was certain that it was a hoax, but saw no angle on setting up a con on Joanie that wasn't tied into blackmail. I sat to work out the angles, hoping that the drink would help. I had barely started to think when the hostess entered, leading Roscoe Arbuckle. He detoured over, the hostess following.

"May I join you?" he asked.

"Yes, please do."

Arbuckle turned to the hostess.

"Thank you, Miss. I'll sit here."

He sat facing me.

"I'm so glad I found you here. I don't want to be bothered, and thought if I were with you, it would defer the idly curious. Is that all right?"

"Sure. Suit yourself."

Arbuckle got a waiter's attention.

"I already ordered Scotch and soda," I said, "but if you'd like something else..."

"No, that's fine," Arbuckle said as the waiter was returning with the drinks I had ordered earlier.

"Please bring more of the same," he said to the waiter.

We raised our glasses to each other before taking a drink. Arbuckle smiled congenially.

"So, what are you working on?" Arbuckle asked.

"I'm retired."

"You must be working on something."

I looked at him over the rim of my glass. Behind him the dining room staff was preparing to dress the room for dinner. Carts full of linen and silverware were wheeled in and parked in various places around the room. Carts of the more formal floral centerpieces were brought in. Poinsettias, evergreen garlands, and holly sprigs were being checked and replaced. More mistletoe was hung up over the dance floor. Arbuckle continued speaking.

"Each trip I've made up or down the coast, you've been here."

"I'm enjoying the scenic view and western ambiance."

He narrowed his eyes a bit at me.

"I would have bet you were working a case."

"Everybody always thinks that. It's an occupational hazard. But what about you? What's on your mind?"

He looked around the club's interior. At this afternoon hour, the crowd was thin. The staff outnumbered the patrons.

"I'm thinking that if I were to help someone who is in a bit of a jam, the publicity would be good for me."

I downed the remainder of my drink.

He used the lull in our conversation to lean in close to me. Looking both ways, he lowered his voice to signal confidentiality.

"You wouldn't know of something nefarious about to happen, would you?"

"Contrived events rarely play out as planned."

"But how can I find someone who needs help?"

I motioned to a waiter who came over.

"Could we get some bread and butter?"

"I'm sorry sir, but the kitchen is closed for an hour between the end of lunch and the beginning of supper. It won't be long now until the kitchen reopens."

"That's okay. I can last until supper."

The staff began decorating the tables for the evening's festivities. The crews were efficient, each person with a different task. They stripped off the afternoon linens and spread fresh tablecloths. Place settings were laid in front of each Bentwood Chair. Silver-and-gold-edged napkins folded in the shape of Christmas trees stood atop of each stack of plates, with the gold-rimmed bread plate on top, the matching salad plate next, and the large dinner plate on the bottom. Silver carafes for coffee and tea remained on the carts awaiting their time to serve.

I turned to Arbuckle.

"Places like this sometimes have a blackmailer who preys on the indiscretions of others. If someone helped expose a blackmailer, that could be a feather in his cap."

"Are you saying..."

"Not really. I was just trying to help you imagine the potentialities."

I finished my drink. The smaller tables for two or four people held small centerpieces of red and white roses mixed with evergreen branches and pine-cones. The tables for six and eight were decorated with larger ones, and the grand table that anchored the northern end of the room had two large Christmas-themed floral centerpieces.

"I could spend a few days here and see if I can scare up any action."

"If you want to generate scandal," I said, "you'll need a woman to play along."

He glanced around the room, perhaps looking for prospects.

"Do you have any suggestions?"

"I may know just the right one. She's part of San Francisco's society set. That would make both of you potential targets."

"And give us a better chance of catching the blackmailer," said Arbuckle.

Torres' nephew Contina was playing traditional holiday music on the piano, all slow- or moderate-tempo.

"Let me see what the lady says. If she's game, she'll have supper with you tonight."

Arbuckle looked thoughtful.

"You know, this could make a great two-reeler plot. I'll call it *Once a Hero*."

He focused on me.

"I look forward to having supper with your lady friend."

"Confidence looks good on you. Keep it up."

"I'm sure I will."

We dangled, giving the restaurant crew a chance at our table. I went looking for Mrs. Miller. I found her sitting in the sun on the bluff-side of the Roadhouse.

"I may have found a cure for your boredom," I said when I was near.

She looked up.

"I could use a cure. That card game you had me watch was a bust. What do you have in mind now?"

I sat on the chair next to her.

"How about some flirting with Roscoe Arbuckle?"

"*The* Roscoe Arbuckle?"

"He's hoping to attract the attention of a blackmailer that may be operating here."

"You set me up on a blind date with a movie star?"

"If you're interested, you can take your supper with him this evening."

"I'll be there with bells on, and I take back all the bad things I ever said about you."

She slipped her fingers under the edge of my sleeve, her diamond rings sparking in the light.

"That leaves us a few idle hours before I have to dress for dinner," she said.

"You're insatiable."

"It's about time you noticed."

Chapter Twenty-Five

I returned to the Casino where I found George Whittell, Jr. actively engaged with a dish of brunette. The two were oblivious to their surroundings, with the woman playfully nipping Whittell's nose after dangling mistletoe between their faces.

"Who's the chippy with Whittell?" I asked the bartender.

"That's Anna Philbrick, the Head of Housekeeping."

"Do tell," I said while observing the previously unnamed woman I had seen with Cayte in the Casino my first night.

The pieces were beginning to fall into place.

Whittell wore a neatly tailored Navy Blue suit with gold buttons. His cravat was gold over a pale blue silk shirt. His shoes were black Oxfords.

Anna Philbrick wore a Forest Green satin gown whose long lines accentuated her trim figure. The back was open, showing her smooth alabaster skin from her shoulders to her waist. I couldn't see her shoes from where I sat. She wore her hair in the shorter style of the day. Her shoulder-duster emerald earrings looked extremely expensive. They sat at a side table near the bar, sharing a pitcher of what looked to be Martinis.

I settled in at the bar, keeping an eye on Whittell and Philbrick. They were in no hurry, except to get to know each other better. She touched his face and then laughed, a tinkling laugh like a celeste. It would have been difficult to distract him from her.

I was working on my third Rye and soda when the lovebirds fluffed their wings for flight. They went out the front, and I followed. Fortunately, they were too interested in each other to notice me, helping with my tail-job.

I followed them through the supper club where Ory's Orchestra was playing tunes for the evening's dancers. I scanned the room and saw the Miller widow and Arbuckle sitting together while the staff cleared their dessert plates and served coffee. They seemed to be enjoying after-dinner drinks while listening to the music.

Whittell and Philbrick continued on to the breezeway, and up the stairs. I hung back for a moment, and then followed them up. At the second floor, I stopped and listened. Philbrick's carefree laugh floated down the hallway. I went after them.

At the middle stairs, they continued past the ashtray room that Cayte had shown me and stopped at the next room. Philbrick produced a key and made to unlock the door. I faded down the stairs and listened.

After some giggling, they went inside and shut the door. I went back into the second floor hallway and walked to the second room. I listened at the door. The two lovebirds were just getting started.

I retraced my steps to the first room, the one that Cayte called "the ashtray room." Looking both ways, I saw no one, so I pulled my gat, and used it to rap on the door. After a minute, I knocked again.

The door opened. A young man of short build stood there. I showed him my gun. He backed into the room. I followed him in and closed the door behind me.

He was a small-boned man of medium height. His hair was blond and smooth. His hands looked soft with long tapered fingers and no rings. He was a pretty one. Maybe he had a future in pictures.

"Who are you?" he blurted.

"Close your yap."

Keeping my gat stuck in his face, I frisked him one-handed. I relieved him of his wallet, keys, and a two-shot .22 caliber Derringer. He wore black pants and a pink shirt, open at the collar. His shirt-sleeves were rolled up, as if he was ready to work on something. His breathing was rapid and shallow.

I pointed to the couch.

"Sit down."

He sat on the end away from me. His eyes kept darting to where I knew the cameras were. I wondered how many he had rolling at this point.

I picked up the telephone. I got the operator to connect me to the confidential line of the American Detective Agency. I took the chance to give a few quick glances around the sitting room. An open carton of Chesterfield Kings sat on the couch table. Next to it was an ashtray with two butts in it.

"Prospects Unlimited, may I help you?"

"Yeah, I need a pickup at the Roadhouse in Half Moon Bay, Room 214."

"The Roadhouse in Half Moon Bay, Room 214. We'll be there as soon as we can."

I hung up the phone and focused on the little man.

"I know all about the blackmail racket that you're running here. What I want to know is who you are doing it for. Does Torres know about your little operation?"

"No, Mr. Torres is unaware of this. Who are you?"

"I work for the American Detective Agency. One of our clients had his life ruined by your little blackmail operation. I'm here to fix that."

"I'm not talking. Go ahead and take me in. I'll do my time."

"You're not hearing me clearly. I don't care about you. I'm ready to kill you, but not before we work out how much pain you can take. Maybe you can convince me that you should live."

That shook him. A worried look hung on his face.

"That's right," I said. "You'll be dead. All your dreams for the future will be moot. Your friends will never learn what happened to you. If you give me what I want, then you can live."

I looked in his wallet for his identification. I watched his eyes as I spoke.

"Manolis Raptis. Now there's a Greek name. You live in Millbrae."

He didn't react to what I was saying.

"I've already searched this room. The stash of blackmail material is somewhere else. Maybe your place in Millbrae?"

"There's nothing there."

He fidgeted, looking worried. His eyes were wide, and his forehead was sweating profusely. His armpits were starting to wet.

"I think I'll stop by there and see what I can find."

"I live with my mother. I tell you, there's nothing there."

I waved my gun for effect. He flinched every time the gun pointed at him.

"How can I be sure? I need to find what all you have on my client. Maybe I should interrogate your mother to see what she knows."

"My mother knows nothing about this. Look, I'm doing this for a cause. I'm sorry about your client, but we need the money. So we soaked a few rich folks. So what?"

"It's not about the money; it's about the threat of exposure."

The Greek tried to reason with me, arguing his case as if I were a judge.

"I know all about that."

I waited, my gun still on him.

"I'm.. a pansy."

"What's that got to do with blackmail?"

"For the last decade, the Police have been stepping up their enforcement of sodomy laws, prosecuting us for our private lives. It's not fair. We use the money to protect us against these infernal prosecutions."

"Blackmail isn't fair, either," I said. "You get the goods on what people do in their private lives and then extort money from them to pay lawyers to protect what you do in your private lives. Hypocrisy is what that is called."

"So what? They can afford it."

"You know that this can't go on. I don't care about you, your friends, your politics, or what you do in the future, but the extortion of money from my client will cease. Now, where is the blackmail stash?"

He turned toward me with a belligerent look on his face.

"I can see you need some convincing."

I hit him in the face with my pistol.

He cried like a baby. He held his face in his hands, tenderly, on the right side.

The hands on the wall clock marched across the clock face counting the mere seconds that the beating was taking so far.

"There's more of that coming if you don't tell me where the goods are."

I left-hand slapped him across the face for good effect.

He cried some more.

I didn't feel sorry for the punk. He was in over his head, only he didn't know it. Just a kid trying to play tough.

"Look, we both know where this is going. You play the brave guy, I beat you more, and eventually you give up the goods. Just tell me the location now, and you can save yourself from the beating, and maybe save your good looks for your boyfriends."

He looked up at me with tear-filled eyes.

"If I tell you, you'll let me go?"

"Yes."

"Then you'll find what you want in the Cheshire Real Estate office on Montgomery Street in Millbrae. It's all in a safe. The combination is 49 right, 21 left, 38 right."

I wrote the combo on an envelope and stuffed it back into my pocket.

"Now can I go?"

"No way, José. I need to verify that the bindle I want is there."

"Then what are you going to do with me?"

"I have a couple of my friends coming to pick you up for safe keeping. If your story is jake, then you're free to go. Just don't try the same pinch again. We're shutting this one down, and if you have backup copies, you'd better give them up now, too."

"No backups. It's all in the safe."

"Are you sure? Because next time I'll shoot you dead as soon as I see you."

"I told you: no backup copies."

"Good. Now why don't we just relax until the Cavalry arrives. You got any liquor?"

"I've got a bottle of Rye and some soda in the cabinet. No ice."

"That's a good start toward being *amigos*. Pour us both a drink and we can toast to a better future while we wait for my *compadres* to arrive."

About two hours later — without another word from the boy — there was a knock on the door. I opened it to see Sean McGervey and Joe Goetz standing in the hallway. I walked deeper into the room while they followed.

"This is Manolis Raptis, and he's ready to be babysat while I get the blackmail stash. I'll send word on how it goes."

I gave Raptis' wallet to McGervey.

"Don't let him out of your sight.

McGervey nodded in agreement.

I turned to Raptis and held up his keys.

"I'll keep these to get into the Cheshire Real Estate office. You can have them back after I'm done."

He gave a grunt.

"Let's go," Goetz said.

Chapter Twenty-Six

*I*t was some time after midnight, nearer to 1:00 when I arrived at the Cheshire Real Estate office. It was in a building sandwiched between a diner and a florist. I peered through the closed blinds: the office looked unoccupied. I found the key that fit and entered. The front area had a receptionist desk. On the other side was a lavatory. In the middle of the two was a wall with a door. I searched the desk and found empty drawers. I glanced into the lavatory and noticed that the toilet paper roll was empty.

I went through the door into a back area. There were two offices with their doors open, and in between was an office with a locked door. A quick search of the open offices yielded nothing.

I returned to the locked office and found a key on Manolis' ring that fit the locked door. I entered. The smell of darkroom chemicals, various silver halide compounds, and thiosulfate solutions greeted my olfactory nerves. I made my way through to the back where I found a safe. A quick reconnoiter proved it to be the only safe in the suite.

It was a squat metal cube, about three feet high and just as wide, set on steel wheels made for metal track. The top and walls were smooth. The door had a round wheel for moving the tumblers and a handle for moving the locking mechanism. *Holdfast Safe* was printed on the door.

I pulled the envelope I was using for my notes. I tried the combination that Raptis gave me.

It didn't open the safe, even on a second try.

I returned to the front where I stuck my head out the door and gave a whistle.

A couple of Brian O'Doul's lads popped out of the cab of a Mack truck while another jumped off the back.

"Grab the gear," I hollered. "We've got a safe to move."

I showed them the safe in the darkroom.

"How are we supposed to get it out of here?"

"I'm the detective; I found it. Getting it to our warehouse is your problem. Don't harm anything taking it out."

"Easy for you to say."

"Natcherly," I quipped.

Chapter Twenty-Seven

I returned to the Roadhouse. It was just before 6:00 a.m. I went to the Front Desk anyhow.

"Is Mr. Torres busy?" I asked the desk clerk.

"I'll check."

He picked up the desk phone and pushed a button. He conferred with the party on the other end before turning to me.

"Mr. Torres will see you. His office is up the stairs..."

"I know the way."

I knocked on Torres' office door.

"Come in."

I entered.

Torres was pouring himself a cup of coffee.

"Want some?"

"Sure. I'm always up for a cup of your Joe."

He poured me a mug and handed it to me.

"Are you ever going to come clean with me?"

"Now that I've got a good one for you."

"Let me guess. You've been working a case at my Roadhouse since you got here, and now you want to tell me about it. That means you want something from me."

"I just want to share the fun part. All the legwork is done. Maybe you'll want a piece of the excitement."

"Stop teasing me and spill it."

"Did you know that you had a blackmail racket operating out of here?"

"In my joint? Impossible!"

"No, very possible. I don't know how big it is yet, but the Old Man has a client who paid for it to end. Are you okay with that?"

"Yes. That's money that should have been going to my tables. Instead, the pigeons who were clipped would stay away, and even warn their friends off."

He spat on the floor.

"I hate guys that take money out of my pockets."

"Then here's what I got for you: we snagged the filmmaker and have him on ice, but not his tootsie here at your joint. She's in the dark about us grabbing her guy. Last night we grabbed the safe from a flop-spot in Millbrae and moved it to our warehouse in south city. You're an ex-yegg. Are you up for some of your old line of work?"

"Safe-cracking?" Torres laughed. "Sure, I'll be the can-opener. Where you got it?"

"Hold your horses. We need some ground-rules."

"Okay, what are the table stakes?"

"We got the safe, and you've got yegg skills. That's a fair trade. Next, I tell you who the bim chiseler is that was operating here, and you take care of her. After we crack the safe, we can split whatever cash we find, but all the film and pictures we keep."

"That sounds fair. When do you want to do this?"

"How about now?"

"Sure, what I had planned for today can keep."

I gave him directions to the warehouse and made to leave.

"Hold on," Torres said. "Who's the bird who set up the pigeons?"

"Anna Philbrick…"

"The Head of Housekeeping?"

"And it looks like your nephew will need a new part-timer, if he wasn't in on the clipping himself."

Veins stood out on the side of Torres' head: so, his Latin blood was hot at learning who was the Judas in his fold. After a moment, Torres was calmer. He spoke in his regular tone of voice.

"Don't you worry about the kid: the Continas are family. I'll take care of him."

"And the Philbrick dame?"

"She lacks protection from the consequences of her actions."

"The actions that you know of. Maybe she wasn't dizzy enough to mix everything that she has on your game in with what's in the safe. She might have held something back as protection."

"She will be dealt with."

"And you should remove the cameras in room 214."

"Don't you worry about me; this isn't the first dance I've been to. I'll have the angles covered."

Torres drained his coffee cup before he locked the center drawer of his desk, pocketed the key, and came around to my side.

"Now, how about us getting to the warehouse and cracking the golden egg?"

"I thought you'd never ask."

Chapter Twenty-Eight

The warehouse was in an industrial section of the south city. Brick *façades* covered concrete walls that enclosed concrete slab floors. Regularly spaced windows let natural light into the Gold Rush era structure, originally built by 49er Daniel Gibb, who was active in San Francisco's civic and commercial affairs. The 1906 Earthquake and Fire left it extensively damaged, but it was rebuilt. Twenty-four years later, it was just another warehouse building surrounded by more of the same.

I parked my flivver just before noon and went in to the office, where Brian O'Doul greeted me.

"I'm seeing you needing a coffee."

"Your eyesight is fine."

I went to the coffee mess and grabbed a mug off the stack. The java was dark and strong.

"Sugar?" O'Doul asked.

"Not this morning. Maybe tonight."

"Does she know about it?"

"It's a work in progress."

"Where's our yegg?"

"Torres? He left Half Moon Bay after I did. He'll be along."

We made small talk until Torres pulled up in a sleek Packard. As he hefted a large leather case from the trunk, we went to greet him.

"Nice ride up the coast?" I asked.

"Sure. I just hope it's not a trip for biscuits."

"You pays your money, you takes your chances," O'Doul replied.

"Let's get started," I said.

O'Doul took us into the main warehouse and into a side room where the safe sat in the middle of the floor. A few chairs were in one corner.

"You're in luck," Torres said. "It's the same kind of safe they cracked in the Cornhill Robbery back in 1865. This won't take long. We'll use wedges on the door to force it open."

"I have things to do," said O'Doul before he turned and left.

I got a chair and watched the show. Torres examined the door panel, feeling the seam between the main panel and the door frame. He took a small chisel, tapping it with a ball-peen hammer at the top of the door.

"The trick is to go slow and steady, making a little progress with each pass," Torres said. "It's actually faster to take your time."

"That sounds Zen."

"Maybe. What do I know from that?"

After a few more passes, he worked three wedges into the door, one on each corner and one in the middle. He gave each wedge a few taps with the ball-peen and then repeated. He added two more wedges to the door frame and then made the circuit, hitting the wedges with more force than before.

I was having a fine time enjoying Torres' improvised anvil chorus when a metal-rending sound came from the box.

"That will be the screw threads stripping out."

After a few more minutes of banging on the safe, the door swung open. I stepped forward to look over his shoulder. Torres picked up two bundles of C-notes; he gave me one and pocketed the other.

"I guess it wasn't a trip for biscuits after all."

There were stacks of smaller bills that Torres moved to the top of the safe. He rummaged through the letters and papers that were also there, but found no more money.

"Move over and give me a chance," I said. "How's about you counting the loose money on top while I look for what I came for?"

"Deal."

Torres stood and started counting.

I knelt in front of the safe, pushing letters and papers away, hunting for photographs. None was in sight. One compartment of the safe was locked.

None of Raptis' keys fit. The locked compartment wasn't very strong, but neither was I the best safe-burglar in the West.

"Hand me your hammer and chisel."

Torres passed me the tools and went back to counting money.

It took a lot of beating to get it open.

What I wanted was there: a thick sheaf of negatives and a stack of prints, just waiting to be seen.

I started to run through the prints, hunting for the Spreckels boy's pictures. I found the ones I was looking for. The snaps were pretty bad. Adolf Jr. was definitely enjoying himself, which was good for the blackmail but bad for Alma Spreckels. Bad, that is, until we got our mitts on the photographs. We would get rid of them, which was good for the Spreckels clan.

"How do you want to handle the blackmail victims?" I asked Torres.

"I want to never let it out that people were blackmailed at my Roadhouse."

"And I want to let each victim off the hook gently, getting some good will for my Agency."

I extended my hand.

"So we can shake on protecting the victims?"

"Yes."

Torres' grip was strong, like mine.

He pointed to the two piles of bills.

"There's the loose money split in two. You pick which half you keep."

I reached for one while he scooped up the other.

"It looks like my work here is finished," he said while packing his tools. "I can show myself out."

"Let me walk you to the front. I need to call it in to the main office."

At the door, we said our goodbyes. O'Doul came out of his office.

"Did it go well?"

"Yeah. Call the Old Man and let him know that we got the Spreckels kid's pictures, along with a whole lot more."

"It will take some mean leg-work to track down the other victims, to let them know to stop paying the pinch."

"That's what the Old Man has your crew of youngsters for. Me, I'm retired again."

Chapter Twenty-Nine

*I*t was early evening when I returned to Torres' Roadhouse. When I walked into the supper club, I espied the Miller widow dining with Roscoe Arbuckle. They had a small table to the side, that could hold four people. The evergreen, pine-cone, and floral centerpiece had surrendered two of its rosebuds: a red one was in Arbuckle's buttonhole; a white one behind Mrs. Miller's right ear. I went to greet them before taking a seat at another table of my own, but they wouldn't hear of it.

"I insist that you take your supper with us," Arbuckle said.

"Thank you, I will."

Joanie reached for Roscoe's hand and entwined their fingers.

The hostess gestured to a waiter who came to take my order. After dispatching the waiter, we started in on catching up.

"Why were you gone for so long?" Joanie asked. "We haven't seen you since yesterday afternoon. Where have you been?"

"Here and there. I've been catching the blackmailer and busting into his safe. Sorry to spoil your publicity stunt, Roscoe."

"That's quite all right," Arbuckle said. "It's how the cookie crumbles."

He gave Joanie a special look, who returned the same.

"So, is the blackmail wrapped up?" Mrs. Miller asked.

"Almost. I caught the blackmailer, which is why I was here at the Roadhouse, but there's still a lot of gumshoe work left to finish it. That's for the young detectives."

I paused and gave them an inspection stare.

"It looks like something worked out for you two as well."

"Why, yes. Thank you for introducing me to Joanie. She's a gem of a woman."

The Miller widow blushed as she put a hand on my arm.

"We had a lovely time together."

"Roscoe, I'm sorry that we didn't generate any material for your *Hero* film, if that was your intention."

"I'm very pleased with how things turned out. I haven't felt this relaxed in a long time."

He smiled at Joanie, who smiled back.

We made small talk for the rest of the meal. Midway through, Roscoe excused himself for a bathroom break.

Joanie leaned over and said, "Roscoe was fun, but he leaves in the morning. You and I have unfinished business."

She paused and searched my face. She touched my hand and repeated her trick of a finger inside my sleeve, rubbing below my wrist.

"Maybe we could get together and work out our differences, like I like?"

Her raised eyebrows left no confusion as to her meaning.

Roscoe was returning to the table when I said to Joanie, "Maybe so."

I skipped dessert to go write my report. Roscoe insisted that he pick up the tab for us all. I let him.

I unlocked my hotel room door and entered. I walked through the front room, and thought it felt chilly. The windows were closed, but I could see the breath in front of my face. The leaves and petals of the Poinsettia on the table seemed to quiver. I continued past the bathroom to the bedroom.

As I was retrieving my belongings from the drawer of the Gentleman's valet to put them in my luggage, I caught sight of something in my peripheral vision. I turned slightly to my left. On the bench in front of the mirrored vanity sat a young woman. I stopped, my hands full. When I looked directly at the bench, no one was there.

I walked to the vanity, leaned slightly down, and looked in the mirror. I saw the room behind me. The Poinsettias were trembling. Again, I felt a slight chill. Something blue flickered by my left shoulder.

My fingers went lax.

My belongings dropped to the thickly carpeted floor.

I whirled around. No one was there. After a moment, I slowly turned back to the mirror.

I waited.

A woman in a blue dress and hat shimmered behind me.

This time, I didn't turn around.

"Cayte?" I said hoarsely.

Her pale face looked at mine in the polished glass.

"But you're dead," I whispered.

I felt the faintest pressure on the back of my neck. I closed my eyes.

"This isn't real," I said to myself. "This must be a trick."

Holding my breath, I opened my eyes again. Over my shoulder, Cayte's un-bruised mouth smiled ever so slightly at me in the mirror. Her fingers came near my face. They brushed my cheek, fleeting as a butterfly's wings. My collar moved. I turned around.

I was alone.

The room was warm. The petals of the Christmas flower on the table were still. I touched my throat.

One of my collar pins was missing.

I couldn't put what had just happened in my report. Nobody would believe it. I chose to swallow the truth.

It took several hours and a few drinks to finish my paperwork on the Roadhouse Affair. I bundled my report and the cash from the safe-cracking into the string-binder envelopes, then laid them in the bottom of the suitcase.

In the morning, I would drive to The City and ditch the rental car, go to the office and drop off my paperwork and report, without a mention of the ghost of the Blue Lady.

Then I would catch a series of trains back to Tijuana.

THE END

Author's Note on
Roadhouse Affairs

When I was 10, my dad introduced me to Dashiell Hammett's Continental Op stories. I was enthralled. I swore to myself that someday I would write mysteries like that. I'm now 55 with five mystery-thriller books at four publishers.

I always wished that Hammett would have brought the Continental Op story arc to some kind of resolution, but as a writer, I can't blame him for dropping the character. The Hollywood compensations were quite attractive when compared to writing for the *Black Mask*. Still, as a reader, I wanted closure for the Op's story arc.

A few years ago, a passion started in me to write an *homage* to Dashiell Hammett, to thank him for what he meant to me as a writer, especially with his Continental Op stories. Taking up the two-story sequence that he wrote in the summer of 1924 — "The House in Turk Street" and "The Girl with the Silver Eyes" — I set my story, *Roadhouse Affairs*, in December 1930.

I wrote it in the murky world of real crime and fiction. Hammett's "Tin Star Joplin" was actually Frank Torres, the real life owner of the Roadhouse, known today as the Moss Beach Distillery. I wrote about his Roadhouse and the Prohibition era excitement that happened there. All sorts of San Francisco society are in the story, along with musician Edward "Kid" Ory and his Orchestra. I brought in Roscoe Arbuckle and Buster Keaton to connect the story to Hollywood, where Hammett went in 1930.

But as J. R. R. Tolkien observed, "the tale grew in the telling." The story follows a detective much like Hammett's Continental Op, but it also tracks the storylines found in the other great works. The phrase "spends his life conjugating the verb "to idle'," and Joanie Miller's game of dice, like Fitzgerald's Nancy Lamar's game of dice, are allusions to F. Scott Fitzgerald's "The Jelly Bean."

I also tip my hat to Raymond Chandler, because when using the *I Write Like* tool to "analyze your word choice and writing style," it consistently tells me that my writing is most like his. I guess that re-reading his books so many times deeply influenced me and that it shows.

I used my understanding of James Ellroy's method of integrating true crime and fiction to achieve the fusion that is *Roadhouse Affairs*.

Roscoe Arbuckle's life was ruined by scandal, as Dashiell Hammett's was ruined by being Blacklisted. My understanding of Hammett's life is one of a loyal American who served in WWI and then re-enlisted in WWII. Like many others at the time, he was a member of the Communist Party, but it was more as a supporter of "the little guy" against the strike-breaking Pinkerton thugs than of any Marxist, Lenin, or Trotsky doctrine. I do not believe that a two-time US Veteran wanted the overthrow of the US Government. He just wanted a fair shake for the American worker.

So, here I am, *homage* in hand, having written it out of love for all the greats I've mentioned. May you mystery aficionados everywhere enjoy it.

About the Historical Frank Torres' Roadhouse
(now Moss Beach Distillery Restaurant)
and the Ghost of the Lady in Blue

During Prohibition, the San Mateo Coast was an ideal spot for rum-running, bootleggers and "speakeasies," establishments which sold illegal booze to thirsty clients. One of the most successful speakeasies of the era was "Frank's Place" on the cliffs at Moss Beach. Built by Frank Torres in 1927, "Frank's" became a popular nightspot for silent film stars and politicians from the City. Mystery writer Dashiell Hammett frequented the place and used it as a setting for some of his detective stories.

The restaurant, located on a cliff above a secluded beach, was a perfect location to benefit from the clandestine activities of Canadian rum-runners. Under cover of darkness and fog, illegal whiskey was landed on the beach, dragged up a steep cliff, and loaded into waiting vehicles for transport to San Francisco. Some of the booze always found its way into the garage beneath "Frank's Place." Frank Torres used his excellent political and social connections to operate a highly successful, if illegal, business. Unlike many of the other speakeasies along the coast, "Frank's Place" was never raided.

With the repeal of the prohibition in 1933, Frank Torres remained in the food service business as one of the most successful restaurateurs along the San Mateo County coast. "Frank's Place," now called The Moss Beach Distillery, still preserves its spectacular view and secluded location above the ocean coves.

The Distillery retains one of "Frank's" former customers as well. Its resident ghost, "The Blue Lady," still haunts the premises, perhaps trying to recapture the romance and excitement of "Frank's" speakeasy years. According to the ghostly Coast-side legend, some 72 years ago a beautiful, young woman met, by chance, a handsome dangerous man and fell in love with him. This sophisticated ladies' man was, say some, a piano player in the bar. The naïve young woman, always dressed in blue, was already married to another, but her unsuspecting husband never knew of the illicit affair. She made many trips to the restaurant to be with her lover. The beautiful lady in blue was reportedly killed while walking on the beach below the restaurant with her lover, who himself was assaulted, but survived. It is at the Distillery that The Blue Lady will be found, searching for her lover.

Many strange events have been documented since that time that can not be explained, such as mysterious phone calls from no one, levitating checkbooks, locked rooms from the inside without any other means of entry, women diners losing one earring and then several of the pieces of jewelry being found in one place weeks later, date tampering with computers, sightings by small children. Moss Beach Distillery is glad The Blue Lady is not destructive with her pranks, and it continues to hear of new events that cannot be explained.

Author Photo, BIO, Website, Amazon Author Page, Facebook, Twitter, & Contact

About Newt

Newt has been a Northrop Grumman Technical Fellow. He sold a classical music composition to the Annapolis Chorale, and is working on two operas, "Sitting Bull" and "Crazy Horse and Custer." He sold his first novel, *How the Strong Survive*, to RockWay Press after it was a finalist in their Annual International Competition. His first novel was also translated into French. He is the author of several other mysteries, and contributor to an anthology. He is about ready to paint a series of paintings so that he can mount another art show.

Newton Love

Newt's Amazon Author Page
Amazon.com/Newton-Love/e/B004ANLJ7G

Newt's Website, with his books & music & more
NewtLove.com

Newt on RockWay Press
Newt @ RWP

Newt's Facebook Page
Facebook.com/newt.love

Newt's Twitter
Twitter.com/newtlove
@NewtLove

Newton CrimeScene
A Place for Readers & Writers of Crime Fiction to Meet
Crimespace.ning.com/profiles/profile/show?id=newtlove

Contact Newt
RockWayPress.com/Contact_Us.php

www.ingramcontent.com/pod-product-compliance
Lightning Source LLC
Chambersburg PA
CBHW070932130626

46555CB00001B/394